"Mr. Herskovitz?" I called, pushing the door closed behind me. "Nathan, are you here?"

Mrs. Paterno had entered before me and was peering into rooms as she went. This apartment, like the other two I had seen in this building, was, from my perspective, backward. You passed the bedrooms first on your way to the kitchen and living room. Mrs. Paterno disappeared down the long, dark hall as I checked out the two bedrooms, the first set up as a study, the second with Nathan Herskovitz's old-fashioned double bed and bedroom furniture, both empty. As I regained the hall, I saw Mrs. Paterno turn into the living room. Then I heard a scream of such horror, such agony, that I froze.

By Lee Harris
Published by Fawcett Books:

THE GOOD FRIDAY MURDER
THE YOM KIPPUR MURDER
THE CHRISTENING DAY MURDER
THE ST. PATRICK'S DAY MURDER
THE CHRISTMAS NIGHT MURDER
THE THANKSGIVING DAY MURDER
THE PASSOVER MURDER
THE VALENTINE'S DAY MURDER
THE NEW YEAR'S EVE MURDER

THE YOM KIPPUR MURDER

Lee Harris

Lee Harris

FAWCETT GOLD MEDAL • NEW YORK

A Fawcett Gold Medal Book
Published by Ballantine Books
Copyright © 1992 by Lee Harris

All rights reserved under International and Pan-American Copyright Conventions. Published in the United States by Ballantine Books, a division of Random House, Inc., New York, and simultaneously in Canada by Random House of Canada Limited, Toronto.

http://www.randomhouse.com

Library of Congress Catalog Card Number: 92-90599

ISBN 0-449-14763-0

Printed in Canada

First Edition: November 1992

10 9 8

For Gunhild
my most enthusiastic reader

How much easier is dreaming pious dreams
Than acting bravely.

> Act I Scene III

Nathan lend? His wisdom
Lies just in this: that he will lend to no man.
> Act II Scene III
> from *Nathan der Weise*
> (Nathan the Wise)
> by Gotthold Ephraim Lessing
> 1729–1781

Acknowledgments

The author wishes to thank Ana M. Soler, James L. V. Wegman, Edith Rogovin Frankel, David A. Biederman, Esq., and Jere Beradino for their invaluable help.

1

I pushed the key into the lock and tried to turn it, but it wouldn't move. I tried left and right; I removed the key, reinserted it, and tried again. No luck.

I pulled the key out and looked at it in the dim light of the apartment building hallway. The key was a Segal, and although I couldn't see the name on the lock, I knew it, too, was a Segal. Segal was a name I had come to know since I started working with aged tenants on Manhattan's West Side. Every apartment had at least one Segal lock in addition to the original house lock the landlord had supplied in an earlier, friendlier time. Many doors also had so-called police locks, a lock that governed a pole set into a floor bracket inside the door to keep the door from being broken down. And of course, everyone had a chain and a peephole. Nice way to live when you're eighty.

I stepped back and assessed my situation. Before trying the key, I had leaned on the bell, banged on the door, and called. Mr. Herskovitz was one of only three tenants left in this decrepit building, number 603 in Manhattan's west Seventies. I thought of them alphabetically: Gallagher (on three), Herskovitz (on five), and Paterno (on six). All three were old, all three had lived in this building since World War II days or shortly thereafter, and all three were holdouts in a bitter fight with a landlord who wanted to empty the building, gut it, renovate it, and rent out the apartments at five to ten times what he had been getting.

It was a situation brought on by New York's rent control laws, laws that went into effect in the forties during the war to prevent price gouging and which were never repealed because . . . well, because no one wants to pay more for something if he can avoid it, and there are many more tenants in New York than landlords, and the city responded to the majority without caring very much about fairness. It's not hard to see why.

But although I was in sympathy with those who said rent control was unfair, I was shocked by the tactics of some landlords, like Metropolitan Properties, Inc., the owners of this building. They had managed to persuade all the tenants but the last three to move elsewhere by giving them cash bonuses and helping them find new apartments that they could afford; well, almost afford. If you've been paying $127 for a two-bedroom apartment, you'll probably have to move farther than Queens or the Bronx to find something similar within your budget.

When Metropolitan Properties couldn't budge Gallagher, Herskovitz, and Paterno, the realty company initiated what can only be called terror tactics. They turned off the heat and hot water. They turned off the electricity and gas. They removed the lock from the door to the lobby, letting in what New Yorkers call "squatters." I won't even attempt to describe what they did in the building. Among other plagues, numerous fires were set in stairwells and empty apartments, and turnout-coated firemen became daily visitors. At the point when all the water was about to be turned off, a fiery but lovable old lawyer named Arnold Gold heard about their plight and took on their case as a *cause*. Arnold Gold's life has been full of causes. Although he has a very busy practice, his wife does not wear a fur coat and his children helped put themselves through expensive colleges, but a lot of people are living better lives because he takes on causes at his own expense.

I met him a couple of months ago, and I've been doing odd jobs for him ever since on a volunteer basis. I'm not rich, but I have a small income that I find comfortable, and I teach one course at a college in Westchester County, about twenty miles from New York and about ten from where I live, so I can afford to do things because I want to, not because I get paid for it.

What I was supposed to be doing this morning was taking Mr. Herskovitz to synagogue. That may seem a bit odd, considering that I'm a former nun, but I'd sort of adopted these three old tenants with a passion. Today was Yom Kippur, Mr. Herskovitz's Day of Atonement, and he dearly wanted to go to synagogue. He had a walk of several blocks on unsteady legs, which I would help to make less painful.

When I had offered to help, I had made the almost mortal error of offering to drive him to synagogue to spare him the walk. He had glared at me for a few seconds before acknowledging my ignorance. Not only could he not ride on Yom Kippur, but this year Yom Kippur fell on the Sabbath, and it was particularly important that he not ride on the Sabbath. I had said I would walk with him.

But he had not answered the doorbell and not responded to my calls. And now the key he had given me only two days ago—"In case something should happen, I couldn't get to the door"—did not turn in the lock.

"Mr. Herskovitz," I called once again. "Nathan? Are you there?"

It was as deadly quiet on the other side of the door as it was on mine. I hated this building. In my heart I could not understand why Gallagher, Herskovitz, and Paterno remained. There were no light bulbs on any floor, and the only light came from the dirty windows at either end of the hall. Paint and plaster were chipping off the walls, the paint in thick flakes whose edges showed numerous layers of different colors, each one representing an era, a once new fashion statement, maybe somebody's dreams of grandeur. Now they lay like so many dried-up leaves that crunched underfoot. Dust balls blew along the stained, patched linoleum, carried by the chill breeze from the broken windowpane at one end. The three occupied apartments were like outposts in a desert. Safety had been, to some degree, restored along with the utilities; Arnold Gold had seen to it that a new, shiny, heavy-duty lock had been installed on the lobby door, but in the evening one heard scurrying sounds, and I chose not to speculate on their origin. And many of the empty apartments still had the leavings of the squatters who had been turned out. Drug paraphernalia lay scattered everywhere, along with the remnants of meals eaten months ago. I had suggested to Arnold that I might clean up at least the apartments adjacent to the three occupied ones, and he had flown into a rage. Not only was it NOT MY JOB TO DO THAT KIND OF THING, but the danger of DISEASE lurked in every piece of garbage. I didn't argue.

Turning away from Nathan Herskovitz's door, I went down the hall to the stairwell and then down to the third floor, maintaining my calm by an act of will I always employed when using the stairs. On three, I walked along a hall identical to the one upstairs until I came to the only closed and locked door. I pressed the bell and heard it ring inside.

"Who's there?" a hostile voice with an Irish lilt called.

"It's Chris Bennett," I called back.

"One moment, darlin'."

I smiled and waited for the sound of three locks opening. "Good morning," I said to the handsome, bathrobed man with a head of hair so thick and silvery that it belied his age.

"And how is my ray of sunshine this Saturday morning?"

I walked inside and listened to the clicks and snaps of the three locks behind me. The smell of fresh coffee permeated the apartment. "I'm worried about Mr. Herskovitz," I said. "I've rung and knocked and called, and there's no answer."

"Well, he's old enough to take care of himself now, don't you think?"

"I'm really worried, Mr. Gallagher. I came to take him to synagogue this morning. Has he been down here today?"

"Haven't seen him."

"He couldn't have forgotten."

"Herskovitz never forgets."

That was true. He was a tough old guy who had survived more than most people ever read about, and although his body had begun to fail him, his mind was sharp. "Then where could he be?"

"Haven't the faintest."

"Did you see him yesterday?"

"Oh yes, we sat on a bench together on Broadway, and he groused and I groused, and he went home before I did."

"Do you think I should call the police?"

"What, to break down the door? And leave Herskovitz to pay for a new one? Hah."

"What if he's sick?"

Mr. Gallagher shrugged. "Use the phone then. But keep me out of it."

I went to the phone, ready to call 911, but the image of the door to the Herskovitz apartment being battered down troubled me. "I don't suppose you have a key to his apartment," I said, just throwing it out with little hope.

He raised his head and looked upward. "She does."

"Mrs. Paterno?"

"Yup."

"Well, let me ask her."

"Don't say I told."

"I won't. See you later."

I went back to the stairwell and climbed the three flights to six. The hallway was a carbon copy of the other two I had walked along this morning, open doors with ragged holes where locks used to be, dirt, chill, shadows, waste. I stopped at 6G and rang the bell.

"Who's there?" Mrs. Paterno called, with more fear than hostility in her voice.

"It's Chris."

The door opened, and Mrs. Paterno stood before me like a black knight. She was a striking-looking woman, tall, dark-haired with only a whisper of gray, aristocratic. Today she was wearing a black jumpsuit and black turban that emphasized her height. As always, there was an air of timeless classiness about her. Of the three tenants, she was the one I could least understand as a holdout.

She said, "Good morning," but didn't ask me in. She never did.

"You wouldn't happen to have a key to Mr. Herskovitz's apartment, would you?" I asked.

"Why?"

"I came to take him to synagogue, but he doesn't answer and I'm worried."

She pulled the door open, allowing me in, then quickly closed the door. I heard the snap and click of two locks.

"What's his number?" she asked, heading for the kitchen.

I told her and she dialed. She stood there with the phone, a long black column, with her chin tilted upward. Finally she hung up. "There's no answer."

"I know."

"Perhaps he's gone for a walk."

"I don't think so, Mrs. Paterno. I was to come for him at nine, and I was a few minutes early. If you don't have the key, I'll call the police and have them break the door down." I turned to leave.

"Wait." She opened a kitchen drawer and pulled out a key ring with two keys on it. They looked just like the ones Mr. Herskovitz had given me. "I need them back," she said. "In fact, I'll go down with you." She put them in her jumpsuit pocket and took her own keys from a handsome snakeskin bag on a kitchen chair.

Outside she locked her own two locks, and we started for the stairs.

"I have Herskovitz's, Herskovitz has Gallagher's, and Gallagher has mine," she explained as we went. "We agreed on that when everyone else moved out."

"Sounds like an interesting arrangement."

"A practical arrangement. Better than everybody having the keys to everybody else's apartment." She said it as though she were talking about a great number of apartments and keys. "This way, if someone's been inside, you know who."

We had reached five and were halfway to Nathan Herskovitz's door.

"I've never used it," Mrs. Paterno said. She stopped in front of D and inserted the Segal key in the Segal lock. It turned easily. Then she used the key to the landlord's lock. That, too, turned and the door opened.

"Mr. Herskovitz?" I called, pushing the door closed behind me. "Nathan, are you here?"

Mrs. Paterno had entered before me and was peering into rooms as she went. This apartment, like the other two I had seen in this building, was, from my perspective, backward. You passed the bedrooms first on your way to the kitchen and living room. Mrs. Paterno disappeared down the long, dark hall as I checked out the two bedrooms, the first set up as a study, the second with Nathan Herskovitz's old-fashioned double bed and bedroom furniture, both empty. As I regained the hall, I saw Mrs. Paterno turn in to the living room. Then I heard a scream of such horror, such agony, that I froze.

Mrs. Paterno had found Nathan Herskovitz.

2

There are moments in life that are so hideous, you would agree to pay a stiff penance to eradicate the memory. That's the way it was when I entered Nathan Herskovitz's living room that Yom Kippur morning and saw his body. In a glance, which was all I could stomach before dragging Mrs. Paterno out of the room and leaning against the wall to try to recover my equilibrium, I could see he had been badly beaten. I assumed it was Nathan, although the face . . . Even now I cannot think of it.

Mrs. Paterno stumbled to the bathroom, and I pressed my palms against my ears to block out the sounds of her agony. When she came out, finally, into the hall, she looked older and gaunter. The turban on her head suddenly looked like a foolish, heavy impertinence, not a regal fashion statement.

We left the apartment and returned to hers, where I called the police. I wanted to call Arnold Gold as well, but today was Yom Kippur and I knew he and his wife were going to synagogue. If I was early enough to find him at home, I would ruin his day. I decided to wait and call after nightfall.

I waited downstairs for the police to arrive, which they did very quickly. They were very kind (with the slight exception of a muttered "Christ, why can't they die on two for a change?" as we mounted the stairs) and treated the three of us—Mr. Gallagher came up as soon as I told him—with respect. For most of the time that we were in 5D, we sat in the Herskovitz study, I at the desk, the other two on a very old sofa of cracking brown leather. Mrs. Paterno seemed nearly catatonic. The shock of seeing the body, the bloody carpet, the splattered furniture, draperies, and walls had left her speechless and occasionally trembling, although it was warm in the room. Metropolitan Properties had managed to heat the three occupied apartments, probably at a cost equaling a whole new system, and the heat was abundant.

"You'd think they'd stop short of murder," Mr. Gallagher said with a sigh.

"Who?" I said. "What do you mean?"

"Our friendly landlord, of course."

"You think Metropolitan killed Mr. Herskovitz?"

"They tried everything else, didn't they? Turned off the lights, sent in the addicts, fed the rats a better diet than I eat, tried to burn us out. It didn't work. Gold took them to court and made them spend money they'll never get back. We could live another ten years. Fifteen if we work at it. So you send the goons in and kill a poor old man, and then the others get cold feet."

"I can't live here anymore," Mrs. Paterno said, although I was sure she hadn't heard a word of Gallagher's lament.

"See what I mean? Then there's just me. What should I do? Take a blanket and stake my claim to a piece of floor at Grand Central?"

"I can't believe they would stoop to murder," I said.

"Read the papers, girl." Gallagher sounded exasperated. "It's been done before. Maybe they were just supposed to give him a friendly beating and it got out of hand. You know how it is. You love what you're doing so much, you just can't stop."

I didn't answer. Something was tickling my brain, a question I had to ask Mrs. Paterno. I opened my bag and pulled out a tissue, touching my keys as I searched. Then I remembered.

"Mrs. Paterno, when you turned the key in the Segal lock, was it locked? Did you feel the lock turn?"

She shook her head ambiguously, her eyes vague. I didn't know whether she was answering no or just conveying a lack of knowledge. She had aged a decade since I rang her bell this morning. I had thought she was a well-preserved late fifties. Now she looked a hopeless seventy.

"It was locked," she said in a monotone. "The bottom one, I don't know. The top one was locked."

"Then someone had the key."

She looked fearful for a moment. "I have never used that key before today," she said with fervor.

"I don't mean you, Mrs. Paterno. Maybe someone carried groceries home for him and took the key after killing him."

"A push-in? Not likely," Gallagher said. "Herskovitz carried his own."

"I don't see how. He had his cane. Going up all those steps must have been difficult. If he was carrying something—"

"I thought you got him his stuff."

It was true that I had shopped for Mr. Herskovitz for the last month and a half, and I had carried a rather heavy bag from the supermarket only two days earlier. "He might have needed milk and bread," I said.

"You're reachin', darlin'. You don't want to face the facts."

I truly didn't. The thought of a building owner resorting to murder to empty his building represented the kind of moral low I found difficult to comprehend. Still, I could not ignore what I read in the papers. Such things had been attempted.

"He had children, didn't he?" I said, changing the subject.

Mrs. Paterno raised her eyes and lowered them.

"A girl and a boy," Gallagher said. "Nina, I think she is, and the boy, maybe Mitchell. He didn't talk too much about them."

"Didn't they grow up in this building?"

"Didn't know him then. There were kids by the dozens back in the fifties. Herskovitz and me, we got to know each other when the place started goin' to the dogs."

"Where am I going to go?" Mrs. Paterno said, looking at no one.

"Do you have family?" I asked. Of the three, she had said

the least to me in the two months I had been coming around. Most of what I heard from her was complaints; this isn't working right, that isn't the way it should be. Even when I came to help her or to deliver a message, she never asked me in. She stood on her side of the door, frequently with the chain in place, and I stood in the dark hall like some lesser mortal.

"A daughter," she said, as though that ended the discussion.

"Maybe she can—"

"Impossible."

"Would you like to stay with me for a little while?" For a hundred reasons, I didn't want company, but the poor woman was terrified, and I didn't know what else to do.

"Where do you live?"

"In Oakwood. It's in Westchester County near—"

"I cannot be out of the city." She looked away, dismissing any other offer of help.

"Someone will have to notify his children," I said.

"Look in the drawer," Gallagher said. "He told me once where he kept the addresses. In case anything happened, someone should know."

I opened the center desk drawer, conscious that the police were just down the hall doing their grisly tasks and would probably not appreciate my snooping. They had asked us not to touch anything. There were scissors, pencils, pens, a large rubber eraser, and a bottle of ink. I closed the drawer and tried the top right one. An old leather book with ADDRESSES stamped in gold on the cover met my eyes. I took it out and opened it on the desktop. Under H I found "Mitchell (Carolyn)" as though he had written in his daughter-in-law's name at a time when she was so new to the family that he might forget her name. I copied down the address and telephone number. Mitchell and Carolyn lived in Atlanta, Georgia. There was no Nina in the H's, so I leafed through the book, starting with A, looking for her. When I reached the XYZ page, I realized she wasn't listed.

"His daughter's not here," I said, looking at Gallagher.

"Oh, she's there, all right. Preston, something like that."

I went back to the P's, but the only listings were for an "H. Plotkin" and for "Pharmacy (close)." I was about to give up when I saw something ragged sticking out of the back cover. I flipped over to it and found a piece of paper in the shape of a long triangle, obviously a flap torn off an envelope. Printed on it in raised blue script was "Mrs. Gordon Passman" at an address on Long Island. Under it in ink was a phone number.

"Passman," I said.

"Passman, that's it." Gallagher smiled. "I knew he had it."

I copied down the information, reinserted the envelope flap, and put the book back.

Just as I did, one of the policemen who had climbed the stairs with us came into the room. "Mr. Gallagher? Want to come with me? Detective Sloan would like to talk to you."

Gallagher lifted himself from the couch, gave me a quick smile, and left the room. A moment later, the policeman was back.

"Mrs. Paterno? This way, please."

Mrs. Paterno stood and walked out without looking at me. She had regained her bearing, although her color was still poor.

The policeman returned a moment later. "So how ya doing?" he asked as if we were old friends.

"OK."

He made himself comfortable on the sofa, or as comfortable as he could be with the big leather belt and the holster carrying his gun. "What a way to start the day, huh? Walk in on somethin' like that."

"It was pretty awful," I agreed.

"Poor old guy. You gotta wonder about New York sometimes."

"Yes." I didn't feel chatty, but he went on, and I responded to keep from seeming impolite. Finally a man in civilian clothes popped his head in the door.

"You Christine Bennett?"

"Yes."

"We can talk in here." He motioned to the uniformed officer, who vacated his comfortable perch.

"Would you like the desk?" I asked.

"Sure."

I carried my bag to the sofa and sat. As it happened, I was dressed for an evening dinner date, not having wanted to return home and then drive back into the city. I was wearing a suit of a rather beautiful shade of blue, and black sheer stockings. I could feel the detective's eyes as I walked across the room.

"I'm Sergeant Franciotti. Can you tell me what you were doing here this morning?"

I told the story in abbreviated fashion. For some reason, I didn't mention that Mr. Herskovitz had given me his keys and that they hadn't worked. I think at that point I had pretty much forgotten that part, and later, when I thought about it, I couldn't see that it could mean very much. I told him about coming down to five with Mrs. Paterno, how she preceded me down the long apartment hall, how I heard her scream. I had introduced my story with an explanation of who I was and how I was connected to the three holdouts in the building. The detective had heard of Arnold Gold and made a note of his name when I mentioned it.

I found it amusingly ironic to be questioned in this manner by a police detective. I have what is called in the common parlance a boyfriend, a word I find very distasteful and more suited to high school romances than adult relationships. Jack is not a boy, and he's much more than a friend. He's also a police detective sergeant, working out of the Sixty-fifth Precinct in Brooklyn. I met him in June when I was only a few weeks out of the convent. We clicked, probably too soon and too firmly, and I asked for some time apart, a brief hiatus, if only to convince myself that I'd been right the first time. We hadn't seen each other for a couple of weeks, and that night, under pressure from my neighbor in Oakwood, I was meeting her cousin for dinner in Manhattan. We had spoken on the phone and he sounded very nice, although he must have wondered what he was getting into, taking out a woman who'd spent half her life in a convent. I hoped he would be surprised.

Looking at Sergeant Franciotti, I could imagine Jack at work. As he asked his questions, I kept trying to guess where he was leading me. But as it turned out, he wasn't leading me anywhere. He was just getting times and places and relationships straightened out. The only time he was anything but neutral was when I told him about the key arrangement. His forehead creased and his face curled into something that looked half-skeptical and half-disbelieving.

"Never understand these people who stay," he said. "But they got their rights."

"Has anyone called Mr. Herskovitz's children?" I asked.

"Haven't found anything on them yet."

"I've got their names and addresses. Would you like them?" I handed him my notes.

He wrote it all down.

"Would you mind if I called them?"

"Be my guest. Use the phone in the kitchen. The crime scene guys are done with it."

"Thank you." As I left the study, Sergeant Franciotti was looking at the names in his notebook.

I didn't volunteer because I'm good at this sort of thing or because I like to do it. It just seemed I'd be a better bearer of bad news than a policeman who complained about people dying on high floors.

In the kitchen I dialed the number for Nina Passman. It rang and rang, reminding me again that this was Yom Kippur, and Nina and her family were probably in synagogue. I tried the Atlanta number, but there, too, no one answered. As I left the kitchen, I could hear several people talking in the living room, but I kept away. I had no stomach for the scene.

I went back to the study and told the detective that the Herskovitz children were unavailable, and the probable reason. He said his people would keep trying and that I was free to go.

"Is Mrs. Paterno still here?" I asked.

"She left. So did Gallagher."

"She's very frightened about staying in the building now."

"Yeah, well, I'll have the boys drive around the block here for a while, keep their eyes open. Be pretty safe."

I wondered. "Good-bye," I said.

"Nice meeting you."

I went up one flight to Mrs. Paterno's apartment and rang the bell. There was no answer. I knocked and called, but there was no sound from inside. I wasn't afraid she had met with foul play—the police were a noticeable presence inside and out—but I wondered where she had gone and whether she had a place to stay for the night.

Downstairs I found Mr. Gallagher. He was dressed in worn corduroy pants and a heavy sweater that seemed to top off every outfit. His face was pale, and there was an air of frailty about him that I had never seen before.

"Come and have lunch with me," I said.

"Good idea. Seems safe enough with all the coppers."

"Mrs. Paterno doesn't answer her bell."

"Probably wants to be alone, poor thing."

"I'll check on her later."

We had lunch on Broadway, my treat, and then I walked him home. Then I drove crosstown to where an old friend of mine from St. Stephen's had a small apartment.

3

Sister Celia Rataczak was spending the academic year enrolled in a nursing program at one of the hospitals on New York's East Side. Since St. Stephen's is some distance up the Hudson, she had sublet a tiny, beautifully furnished apartment on First Avenue, which had a sleep sofa in the main living area as well as a bed in a little alcove. We'd known each other for a long time, and I was delighted to have the chance to stay overnight with her after my date this evening.

After I had explained what had happened that morning, I put on a big flannel shirt I had brought along to relax in and hung up my suit jacket and skirt. Celia was wearing the obligatory brown habit of the Order of St. Francis I had once belonged to.

About half an hour after I got there, I finally found someone home at the Passmans'.

When Mrs. Passman came to the phone, I said, "My name is Christine Bennett. I've been helping your father lately, and I'm afraid I have some bad news."

"About my father?" the woman said, and something in her voice made it sound as though there were something preposterous in that.

"Nathan Herskovitz," I said. "I'm afraid he's dead."

There was a silence, and I wished I could touch her, give her support at this terrible moment.

"I think you've made a mistake," the woman said. "My father died twenty years ago."

It took me a moment to recover. I had dialed the right number. She had responded to the name Passman. Had Gal-

16

lagher gotten things mixed up? The envelope had said only Mrs. Gordon Passman. Nothing really identified her as Nina Herskovitz.

"Are you Nina Herskovitz?" I asked.

"I'm sorry. I think you've got the wrong number." She hung up, and I did the same.

"Trouble?" Celia asked.

"I feel like an idiot. I've just called some poor woman and told her her father's dead when her father died twenty years ago. Well, I suppose the police will find the right one. Should I try the son or quit while I'm behind?"

"Give it a try."

I dialed the Georgia number, and a teenage girl answered. I asked for Mr. Herskovitz, and a man said "Hello?" in a voice that sounded almost like Nathan's.

I said it all again and waited.

"He's dead?" the man said. "My father is dead?"

"I'm sorry, yes."

"What hospital are you calling from?"

"I'm not calling from a hospital, Mr. Herskovitz. I've been working with the tenants in his building, and I went down this morning to take your father to synagogue—"

"My father? He was going to temple?"

"He wanted very much to go for the holy day, but he needed a little help walking there." I was starting to wish I had left this for the police.

"My father was going to temple for Yom Kippur?" He sounded more incredulous about that than about his father being dead.

"That's right," I said.

"Excuse me, I didn't get your name."

I gave it to him and explained again what my relationship was to his father and the other tenants. Then he asked me how his father had died.

"It appears to be murder, Mr. Herskovitz."

"Murder. Jesus. My father was murdered?"

"I'm afraid so. The police will be calling you, but I wanted to tell you myself because I was very fond of your father. He was a decent, thoughtful man, and I'm very sorry."

There was a short silence. Then, "Right, right. He was."

"Mr. Herskovitz, I called a Mrs. Gordon Passman, who I thought was your sister, to tell her what had happened, but I seem to have reached the wrong number or person." I gave him the number I had called.

"Yeah, that's Nina's number." He read it back to me.

"She told me her father had died twenty years ago. I really don't understand how—"

"Yeah, well, if you knew Pop and you knew Nina, you'd understand."

"I see. Will you be coming to New York, Mr. Herskovitz?"

"I guess I'll have to. I suppose there are arrangements . . ."

"I'd be glad to help in any way I can." I gave him my phone number and address. "I really mean that, anything at all."

He asked for the name of someone at the police station whom he could call. I gave him Franciotti's name, but I couldn't think of the precinct number. He said not to worry, and I gave him another few words of condolence, and we hung up.

With that behind me, I settled in for a nice talk with Celia.

My date that evening was Mark Brownstein, a first cousin of my neighbor in Oakwood, Melanie Gross. Melanie and I had become friends after I moved into the house I inherited from my aunt Meg, who had lived there about as long as I can remember. Mel had told me that Mark "did something on Wall Street" and was rich and great and good-looking and single. Frankly, I thought it very decent of him to gamble an evening on someone he didn't know, someone who had been a nun for half her life. I assumed Mel had said nice things about me, but even so, I liked his style.

We were meeting rather late, nine-thirty, but as he had explained on the phone, it was Yom Kippur, and he would break his fast with his parents earlier in the evening. (Yom

Kippur, I knew, was a fast day). He also thought it was a great joke that he was concluding Yom Kippur with a former nun.

Celia and I had a pleasant dinner, after which we washed up. I had asked Mark to call for me in the lobby as I didn't want to disrupt Celia's life too much. At nine-fifteen I went downstairs and waited for him.

At exactly half-past, a man came through the door with the doorman.

"Chris?" he asked tentatively.

"Yes. Hello." I held out my hand and we shook.

"I'm Mark. Good to see you."

I could tell by his face that he wasn't disappointed. We went outside and he hailed a taxi.

"We'll go somewhere for a drink," he said, and we chatted until the taxi stopped.

"Somewhere" turned out to be one of those loud, packed, trendy places that I had only heard of. We sat at the bar, ordered drinks, and picked up our conversation.

"Is it top secret why a woman who looks as good in clothes as you do would want to spend her life as a nun?" he asked.

"It's a long story and not very interesting. It has a lot to do with being orphaned at fourteen and coming from a devout family."

"And now?"

"Now I'm a part-time college English teacher and a part-time volunteer for worthy projects."

"Enlighten me."

I did. I told him about Arnold Gold and his causes, about the building he had saved for the tenants. "So I've been helping them out for the last two months, three old people who won't be budged, living in this spooky old building on the West Side, three people who love each other, hate each other, trust and mistrust each other, and ultimately, I'm afraid, can't live without each other. Every time I say their names, I think I'm describing the great melting pot: Gallagher, Herskovitz, and Paterno."

"Melting pot, hell. It sounds like an old-line New York

City election ticket, an Irishman, an Italian, and a Jew. Put 'em together, you'd probably have them running the city.''

"No more, I'm afraid. Mr. Herskovitz was just murdered.''

"Murdered. You've had quite a day.''

"You can say that again,'' I said, reaching for my whiskey sour, which had just been placed before me on a cocktail napkin.

Of course, I had to tell him about it, which I didn't mind doing, because talking about things often clarifies them for me. And he turned out to be interested, which was nice, and then later to be helpful, which was terrific.

"So you went down to take him to temple and you found him dead.''

"That's pretty much it.''

"I guess he wasn't inscribed for blessing in the Book of Life on Rosh Hashanah.''

"You mean the New Year?''

"Right. On both of those holidays you ask God to inscribe you for blessing in the Book of Life. My mother always said, when I was a kid and didn't want to go to temple, that it was something like insurance. You went and put in your good word, and God gave you another year. At least, that's the way I figured it when I was ten.''

"When is the New Year holiday?''

"Last week. Today's Saturday, Rosh Hashanah was a week ago, Thursday and Friday.''

"Mr. Herskovitz didn't go to temple those days.''

"He must've. It's a package deal. You go on Rosh Hashanah, you go on Yom Kippur, and then, if you're the average Jew, you don't go the rest of the year.''

I thought it sounded a little like Catholics and Easter. "Wait a minute,'' I said. "You're right. He asked me for Friday and I couldn't come.'' I took my little date book out of my bag. Arnold Gold had insisted I write down all my mileage and other expenses involved in my volunteer work for some theoretical tax advantage, and although I really didn't know what he was talking about, I kept the records carefully. I opened the book to last week. On the Friday, September 21, rectangle I had written, "Church cleanup two miles." "I was helping out in my local church," I said. "He never said what he wanted me to come in for." I felt a wave of sadness that I had denied Nathan Herskovitz his last chance to attend services.

"Don't let it get you. If he'd really cared, he would have told you what it was all about. How old was he?"

"About eighty, but I never asked."

"Anyway, if I had to make a choice, I'd go with Yom Kippur myself."

The comment struck me as funny, and I laughed. "What happens on these special holidays?" I asked. "I'm afraid I don't know as much about them as I'd like to."

"Well, they blow a ram's horn called a shofar. Not a beautiful sound, but very distinctive. Since it's only on the High Holy Days, it's pretty charged."

"What do you pray for?"

"As I said, to be inscribed for blessing in the Book of Life, to be forgiven for your sins. I'm Reform, and we do the whole thing right in temple, but on the second day of Rosh Hashanah, the Orthodox actually go down to the river and cast their sins in it."

"They what?"

"Figuratively, of course. My grandmother told me about it."

Something came back to me with a rush. "Mark, when I saw Mr. Herskovitz a few days ago, when we made the arrangements for today, I remember he said that in the afternoon, maybe we'd walk down to the river. I assumed he meant he wanted to take a walk in Riverside Park, but that's not how he put it. Maybe he wanted to do the river thing on Yom Kippur because he'd missed Rosh Hashanah. Do you think—?"

"Why not? A man that old might have had a very religious background, even if he wasn't very observant now. He must have been an interesting person."

"He was." I suddenly felt the burden of Nathan Herskovitz's dying without having cast off his sins, of his wanting to make peace in his old age and failing. If only he'd told me how important it was, I'd have given up the church cleanup that day. "I wish I knew more about all this," I said.

"I tell you what. If you come up to my place, I'll show you the prayer book." There was a mischievous glint in his eye, and I knew I was being tested and measured.

"I'd love to," I said, thinking it would have to be quieter there than here.

"They'll never believe this one in the office on Monday morning."

We walked to where he lived. It was a mild night and it felt good to be outside, away from all the noise.

There was a doorman at Mark's building, and the lobby was ultramodern. An image of 603 flashed before me. I hoped what happened to that building would not be repeated here. Time is sometimes very unkind.

Mark's apartment left me almost breathless. The kitchen was a fantasy, and the living room a dream. There were sketches and paintings on the walls, furniture that looked too good to sit on, a rug with an abstract design that I hated to step on. Something that looked like a column from an ancient Greek building provided the touch of antiquity that I supposed balanced all the modern effects.

The contrast between this man and how he lived, and Jack Brooks and his life-style, was so striking, I could hardly see them sharing the same world. Mark was fairly tall and good-looking, his hair cut and styled so precisely that I couldn't imagine it blowing. His suit was cut as though tailored for him, and perhaps it was, the fabric dark with the look of quality, the thinnest, subtlest pinstripe I had ever seen. The watch that he glanced at from time to time was large and gold and had one of those names that you see advertised in the best glossy magazines. Even his tie, which was many shades of blue, spoke of unobtrusive elegance.

Jack Brooks, on the other hand, has curly hair, which I'm sure he thinks of cutting only when he starts to have trouble seeing through it. He has a face that I think is angelic but that, like the rest of him, is rough around the edges. I think it's that roughness that I find so appealing. It speaks of where he comes from and what he's capable of, a toughness that's just below the surface, but always there. I saw it once last summer when my life was in danger, and I was grateful for it. I'm sure Jack could learn to wear five-hundred-dollar suits—anyone can—but I think it would take some mental shenanigans to get him to do it.

Still, I liked Mark, and I was enjoying the evening. We sat in his living room sipping liqueur and listening to music on a compact disc player that was part of a huge sound system, most of it cleverly hidden around the room. He found his holy day prayer book and gave it to me, telling me I could keep it for a while; he would retrieve it when we next met.

Finally I said, "You haven't told me a thing about yourself."

"Not much to tell. I work on what's known as 'the Street,' put in fourteen-hour days, come home and collapse, and have a good time weekends."

"You don't have much time to appreciate your beautiful apartment or cook in that fabulous kitchen."

"But I have a deepening relationship with my microwave. It keeps me from starving."

"I don't even own one," I said.

"You probably don't feed yourself junk food that needs reheating or frozen garbage from the store."

"I'm trying to learn to cook, you know, starting with raw meat and vegetables."

He smiled. "They still grow 'em that way?"

"Maybe not in New York."

We chatted for some time along those lines, conversation that we kept light and fun. Around midnight I said I ought to be getting back to Celia's. Although I offered to take a taxi myself, Mark accompanied me, and at Celia's door, he gave me a good-night kiss. When I was inside and had locked Celia's two locks, I thought it would be nice to get Jack a good silk tie for Christmas.

Against one wall in Celia's tiny kitchen was a small table

with two chairs. She had left the light on in there to help me find my way around. Since the kitchen was around a corner from her sleeping alcove, the light didn't disturb her. I sat at the little table and opened Mark's prayer book. Much but not all of it was English on the left page and Hebrew facing on the right. I read some, scanned some, finding it interesting and often moving. The lines he had quoted to me appeared for both holidays, slightly abbreviated for the New Year. But I could see how his ten-year-old self had felt he had made a "deal" with the Almighty by reciting the prayers. The worshiper confessed to having sinned and then asked for a year of happiness, peace, and health. While it did not mirror the Catholic in the confessional, it struck familiar chords.

One sentence made a strong impression on me, and I copied it into the little steno notebook I keep in my bag: "Thou desirest not that the sinner shall perish in his sin but that he shall turn away from his evil and live."

Nathan, I thought silently, was that why you wanted to pray on this Yom Kippur? Was that why you wanted to cast your sins in the river?

4

The Sunday *Times* buried the story of Nathan Herskovitz's murder deep in the first section. The building in which he lived merited more coverage than his life or death. There was a strong sense of looming evil concerning Metropolitan Properties, which "did not answer the phone," and a Bertram Finch, listed as one of the partners, "who did not return phone calls." But there was no overt speculation on who had done it. An unnamed police official said only that "suspects were being interviewed."

I went to mass with Celia and then drove home to Oakwood. I live in a small house with three bedrooms upstairs and a one-car garage separated from the house. Compared to the tiny room I had at St. Stephen's, it's a palace. I took over the master bedroom as my own and fixed up one of the other two bedrooms as a study. I'm teaching a course called Poetry and the Contemporary American Woman at a nearby college and having the time of my life. Since the semester had barely begun, I had, as yet, no papers to correct, although I had already assigned one for mid-October. But the preparation for the class had been a blissful experience of reading four centuries of poetry and planning lectures and discussions on their relevance to modern living.

I was on my way upstairs to put the finishing touches on my Tuesday class when the phone rang. Caught halfway, I decided to take it on the second floor. I answered on the third ring.

"Is this Miss Christine Bennett?"

"Yes, it is."

"This is Mitchell Herskovitz. I hope you don't mind my interrupting your Sunday."

"Not at all. I'm glad you called. Can I help you with anything?"

"I hope so. I flew up this morning, and the police have given me the royal runaround. This Sergeant Franciotti is off today, and no one seems to know what happened to my father, where the body is, when it'll be released, or anything like that. I'm sitting in a hotel room, it's Sunday, and I don't know where to turn."

"Let me give you a number to call." I told him about Arnold Gold, whom I had called yesterday afternoon. If anyone knew his way around the bureaucratic maze in New York, it was Arnold.

"You think I can call him today?"

"I'm sure of it."

"Uh, I'm very grateful for your call yesterday. If I'd waited to hear from the police, I'd probably still be waiting. I talked to my sister afterward. She's sorry for what she said, but her relationship with my father wasn't exactly friendly."

"That's all right."

"You're the one who found him, aren't you?"

"I and one of the other tenants in the building."

"Could we have dinner tonight and talk?"

There was nothing I wanted to do less than drive back into the city, but I wanted to talk to him, too, and I couldn't leave the poor man alone under the circumstances. "I'd be glad to."

He mentioned a restaurant and asked me to be there at six. I agreed, we rang off, and I changed my clothes and settled back with a book and my notes to plan for my next class.

Mitchell Herskovitz was the image of his father, but somewhat taller and about thirty-five years younger. Looking at him and listening to that voice was almost eerie. He was rather ruggedly handsome in spite of thinning hair and a worried frown. Like his father, he wore glasses that tended toward the thick side, but his were more fashionable than Nathan's.

"It wasn't very thoughtful of me to drag you down here. I don't know how far you had to come, but it's very kind of you," he said when we were seated.

"Not far. And I wanted to talk to you, too."

"First off, the lawyer you referred me to, Arnold Gold, he's a real godsend. When I told him I was Pop's son, there was nothing he wouldn't do for me. Seems he knows someone in the district attorney's office, and a couple of hours ago he called back to say they'll release the body tomorrow morning. The funeral will be at two."

"I'll be there."

"I told Mr. Gold I wanted to get into the apartment, and no one at the precinct would give me the time of day. He's taken care of that, too. A policeman will meet me at the apartment tomorrow morning at ten. If you would care to join me—"

"I would."

"Thank you. I haven't been there for a long time, and there are things I'd like to preserve, my mother's things. I'm still feeling kind of rocky, and maybe your presence will ease things a little."

"I'll do whatever I can." Actually, I was glad to be invited. I had not had my wits about me Saturday morning, and I had not had the stomach to take a good look at the living room, where Nathan Herskovitz had been murdered. With the body gone, I thought it might be a little easier.

"Did it look like a robbery to you?"

"Not really. The apartment wasn't messed up." I mentally reviewed the rooms I had looked in. They had seemed as neat as Nathan usually kept them. Certainly the study had not been disturbed. It was harder to say about the living room, where the body had lain. I had only glimpsed it, and although I thought a lamp had been overturned, that could have been the result of a struggle. I didn't have a memory of great disorder. "It's possible they took his wallet, but I don't think they went through the apartment looking for jewelry or cash.''

''Do they have any idea who did it?'' he asked.

''I don't think so. I haven't heard anything.''

''I suppose in New York people get killed for buttoning their coats wrong, and if you're old, it's that much easier to be assaulted, but it's hard to imagine my father the victim of such a violent crime. May I ask you some questions?''

''Of course.''

We ordered first, Mitchell Herskovitz making his selections as though from a list of medically approved foods. He started with fruit, proceeded to broiled fish with no butter, and asked for a green salad with oil and vinegar on the side. After I had ordered, somewhat less cautiously, he began.

''How long have you known my father?''

''About two months.''

''I gathered from the lawyer that it was through him.''

''That's right.''

''Mr. Gold explained about the building and the three remaining tenants. Well, two now. Have you assisted all of them?''

''Yes, I have.'' I wondered where he was going.

''You said you had an appointment to take my father to Yom Kippur services yesterday. Forgive me if I seem dense, but was that your idea or his?''

''It was his idea, Mr. Herskovitz. I didn't even know that day was Yom Kippur till he told me.''

''I can't figure it.''

I decided it was time to ask my own questions. ''What do you find so odd about your father attending services on the holiest day of the year?''

''Because he hadn't done it in living memory. My father had a private war with God that went back fifty years.''

''Would you tell me why?''

''My father was trapped in Europe in 1940. As he told it, he had guaranteed himself a way out, but when he needed it, it was gone. The people who had assured him safe passage were dead or gone themselves or too frightened to help him.

He evaded the Nazis for as long as he could, but he ended up in a death camp. Somehow he survived. He met my mother in a camp for displaced persons in 1945, and they married soon after. I was born there.''

"He didn't talk about it to me.''

"To his credit, he tried to put it behind him. But while he blamed the human beings who created that hell, from the designers of the camps down to the guards who ran it and the railroad engineers who carried people there, he blamed God, too. He said a just God would not have allowed such a thing to happen. He used the Holocaust as evidence that either there wasn't any God, or the God who exists is unjust. In either case, he wasn't about to worship him. Many people who survived the horrors that my father experienced came out of it more religious than before. My father was one of the others.''

"But he told me he was Jewish. He seemed rather proud of it.''

"My father's quarrel was with God, not with the Jews. He saw most of the world as the enemy. Jews were the closest you could come to friends, and even then, you had to be careful. From the look on your face, I'd say you don't believe me.''

"It doesn't sound like the man I knew. I'm Catholic, Mr. Herskovitz. My name is Christine. He called me Christine. He knew what I was even if I didn't spell it out for him. Your father trusted me. I'd venture to say he liked me. He certainly didn't treat me like the enemy.''

"I haven't seen him for many years.'' He shrugged. "Maybe he changed.''

"There were pictures in his living room,'' I said, remembering groups of them on end tables. "They were old and showed a woman and a boy and girl. They must be you, your mother, and sister.''

"She was very pretty, my mother, slim with short hair. She died a long time ago. I always thought the war killed her, but that's probably an excuse. She wasn't very well.''

"There were no pictures of you and your sister as adults," I said.

"I haven't seen my father for a long time." His voice was low.

"And your sister has thought of him as dead for twenty years."

"My sister is very bitter. She and Pop had a falling-out a long time ago. They didn't speak. Nina didn't speak to Pop," he said, as if clarifying his first statement.

"Yom Kippur is the Day of Atonement," I said when it seemed he would go no further. "Can you think of any reason why your father would want to go to synagogue after all these years? Was there something he needed to get off his chest?"

Mitchell smiled. "So many things, I'd have trouble remembering them all."

We dropped the conversation briefly while we ate, and I tried to talk about other things. He showed me pictures of his family and said how much more he enjoyed living in Atlanta than in New York.

"Is 603 the building you grew up in?" I asked after a while. "The one your father lived in?"

"That's the only home he ever had in this country, except for some little place we stayed in when we first came over. I don't remember it at all. My earliest memories are Riverside Park and Broadway. My mother and I used to walk there. On a nice day everyone you knew would be out. Sometimes she'd take me to children's concerts on a Saturday, and every year we'd go to the circus together. She was a lovely person, a wonderful mother."

"I lost my mother, too, when I was quite young. In some ways I never stopped missing her."

"I try to do for my children what she did for me. Except my wife and I do it together."

"You said your father regarded most of the world as his enemy. Could someone out there have been a real enemy with a reason to kill him?"

"How could I know that? I haven't seen him in years. I

don't know anything about him anymore. It's a surprise to me that someone like you knows more about him today than I do.''

"How long has it been since you last saw him?" I asked it quietly, knowing it was none of my business but wanting to know. In the months I had known Nathan Herskovitz, we had talked a great deal, but never once had he mentioned a son, a daughter, a wife, or a life in another country.

"In 1979 my company offered me a promotion if I transferred to Atlanta. My wife and I were ready for a move. We had two small children and an apartment that was bursting at the seams. We were young. We thought this move was just what we needed. I told Pop, and he said . . ." He drank from his water glass. "He said, 'A son doesn't desert his father.' Just that. 'A son doesn't desert his father.' "

"Your mother had died by then."

"Long before that."

"So you did what was best for your family, and he blamed you for deserting."

"That's about the way it was." He drank more water. He was more emotional at that moment than he had been at any other time.

I gave him time to recover and then asked, "Had you been friends with him up to that time?"

"I wouldn't say we were friends. It was hard to be friends with my father. But we got along. We saw each other. We weren't—estranged."

We were drinking coffee by then, and I wanted to start for home. I had declined alcohol because of the drive I had ahead of me, but I am by nature a morning person, and I fade after dark.

"I'll call the other two tenants in your father's building. I'm sure they'd like to be at the funeral. Ian Gallagher and Mrs. Paterno," I added.

"I think I remember Gallagher," he said.

"They spent a lot of time together. If they weren't friends, they were at least very good acquaintances."

"I was able to get an obituary notice in the *Times* and the

Daily News for tomorrow. It'll be interesting to see who turns up. Knowing my father's cronies of years ago, that's the page they turn to first.''

''Will your sister be there?'' I asked.

''She will. And probably Gordon as well.''

I looked at my watch. ''Be sure to call if you need anything at all.''

''I will. This has really been very illuminating. And pleasant. We'll meet at ten tomorrow then.''

I promised him I would be there. Then I drove him back to his hotel and returned to Oakwood.

5

After fifteen years of waking up at 5:00 A.M. for chapel, I am an early riser. I manage to sleep a little longer than that nowadays, and it gets easier as the days grow shorter and the sun rises later, but I was up by six Monday morning. I started the day with a brisk walk, something I will have to give up when the weather gets cold. My neighbor, Melanie, who introduced me to Mark, was not around, but I had no doubt I'd hear from her soon for a report on our Saturday night date. I had intended to call her, but I had come home too late last night.

Jack knows he can reach me in the morning. Just this month he had started his first of what would be four long years of law school at night, so there wasn't much opportunity for evening talk. When the phone rang at eight-thirty, I guessed it might be him, and I was pleased. We hadn't spoken for a while; he was kind of put out when I said I wanted to slow down our fast-moving relationship. Now, having neither seen nor spoken to him for over a week, I was having second thoughts.

"You mind my calling?" he asked with more hesitancy than I had ever heard before.

"Uh-uh. I miss you."

"Well, that's good news."

"How are you?"

"I'm OK. Tired. The reading for my course is unbelievable. You don't do that to your students, do you?"

"No, but I don't equip them for the bar either."

33

"Chris, I want to see you. Are we playing games or is it all over or what?"

"I want to see you, too," I said, ignoring his questions.

"Like when?"

"Like whenever you want."

I swear he breathed a sigh of relief.

"Maybe this weekend," he said.

"Yes."

"You doing OK?"

"I'm fine. I really do miss you."

"We'll do something Saturday." After he said that, I heard his voice and manner change. "I saw something in the paper yesterday, a murder over on the West Side of Manhattan. Was that one of your guys?"

"Yes. One of the other tenants and I found the body." I explained briefly what I was doing there.

"I told you that wasn't a nice place to spend your free time. Those landlords are brutal when they want to renovate and they have holdouts."

"You think it was the landlord?"

"Looks like it. I just talked to a friend of mine at that precinct. They made an arrest overnight, guy named Ramirez, has a sheet a mile long. He's been connected to Metropolitan Properties in the past."

"It's hard for me to believe people can be that cruel."

"They can. They are. I know you don't like to listen to well-meant warnings, but I wish you'd be careful. Like don't go back there. There are other Ramirezes in Metropolitan's stable."

"I have to go, Jack. Gallagher really counts on me, the way Nathan Herskovitz did. Mrs. Paterno is another story, but I'd like to try to convince them both to get out, even if it means accepting a moral defeat."

"There's more at stake here than a moral defeat."

"The sergeant said they'd have the police cars drive around the block for a while. It should be safe."

"Why do I even talk to you? When I hear myself, I sound so damned reasonable. You know, next time you get yourself mixed up in something, I may not be around with an army to bail you out.'' A reference to the last time, when I had thought I would end up dead.

"I'll be as careful as I can. I'm going into the city in a little while. Arnold Gold arranged for the police to open the apartment for Mr. Herskovitz's son. I want to be there.''

"It won't be pretty, Chris, and it won't smell too good. Cops don't clean up. My friend said it was pretty bloody.''

"It was. But Nathan's son wants to get in before he goes home to Atlanta, and I want to look around, too. I'm not convinced your guy Ramirez did it. I talked to Nathan's son yesterday, and Nathan wasn't the sweet old man he seemed to be.''

"Sounds like you're off and running.'' He didn't sound entirely happy.

"I don't know, but maybe.''

We agreed to keep in touch and hung up. It was nearly nine now, and although it was less than an hour to Manhattan, I needed extra time to find a place to park. I put on my new raincoat and set off.

Mitchell Herskovitz was waiting outside the building when I arrived. A minute or two before ten, a car pulled up at the curb. I could see Franciotti inside and another man wearing a suit in the front, but it was a young, uniformed policeman who got out of the backseat. He introduced himself as Officer Schuyler, and we entered the building together.

"I understand an arrest has been made,'' I said as we walked through the lobby.

"No kiddin','' Officer Schuyler said. "I didn't hear nothin' so far. You know who it was?''

"Someone named Ramirez.''

"Oh yeah?'' he said, his voice tipping up. "They got Hey-Zeus for this?'' That's exactly how he pronounced it, slightly stressing the Zeus part.

I must admit to a feeling of depression whenever I hear of someone with that name being arrested for a crime. I think of the man's mother naming her baby son after the Lord himself only to see him end up like this. "You know who he is?" I asked.

"Oh yeah. Real dirtbag. Been around for a long time. We thought he started some fires here a while ago, but we didn't have enough to nail him for it. Maybe now we got him good."

"I hope so," I said without enthusiasm.

Schuyler pulled open the door to the stairs and started up.

"I don't believe this," Mitchell said. "This is how my father lived?"

"The elevators stopped running a long time ago, and even Arnold Gold couldn't get them going again. He was able to get the lights back on and the water running."

"My God," Mitchell breathed.

"Can you make it up to five?"

"I'm in very good shape," he said, although he seemed to be laboring.

The policeman had been holding a flashlight down and behind him to light our way. Since coming to see my tenants, I carried one in my bag, too.

"My God," Mitchell said again. "How do people live here?"

"There are three oases where life goes on more or less as usual. It's just getting to and from them that's a bit unpleasant."

"A bit unpleasant," he echoed softly.

We had reached the Herskovitz apartment. The door was sealed shut with yellow tape a couple of inches wide. I could see where it had been signed, dated, and timed. The name may have been "Sgt. Franciotti," but it wasn't written for easy legibility. The date was September 29, and the time looked like 1835, probably military time for 6:35 P.M. The cops had been there for a good long time on Saturday.

"Listen, folks, I hafta warn you," Office Schuyler said, "you're entering a crime scene. Please try to avoid touching anything, OK? The crime scene guys or the detectives may need to come back, and they don't want any evidence tampered with." He said it all as though he were reading it from a prompt card. He took a key chain out of his pocket, found a small pocket razor knife, and cut the tape. Then he inserted first the Segal key and then the key to the lower lock, pushed the door hard, and pulled the tape away as the door opened.

I followed him in. Mitchell stopped at the study, the first room on the right. "That was my room once," he said. He paused again at the second bedroom, where his parents had slept, but he said nothing. We continued down the hall. I had a terrible feeling of déjà vu, of following Mrs. Paterno on Saturday morning, of hearing her scream.

When we were near the living room, which was slightly around a corner and not visible from the hall, Officer Schuyler said, "I gotta warn you, Mr. Herskovitz, it's not a pretty sight in there."

I followed him in, knowing what I would see but unprepared nevertheless. The beautiful Oriental carpet that covered the floor had been soaked with Nathan's blood. The chalk mark that had been drawn around his body was remarkably small. His body had crumpled, not fallen flat. Hardly anything in the room had been spared the splattering of his blood. The walls, the furniture, the precious objects he kept on the tables, all were marked. His hat still lay where it had rolled when he fell dead.

I turned to look at Mitchell, who had been only a few steps behind me. His face was ashen, and he had started to weep.

"I'm sorry, sir," the policeman said, and I felt myself warm to him.

I touched Mitchell's arm. "Would you like to sit down in the kitchen?"

"No. I'm fine." He pulled a handkerchief out of his pocket and wiped his face. "What's all that white stuff?" he asked.

"That?" Schuyler said, pointing. "Fingerprint powder. You'll find it all over, light powder for the dark surfaces and dark powder for the light ones. See, it's the way the fingerprints show up. They dusted the whole apartment."

"It's the pictures I want."

"I guess that's OK. I'll make an inventory list. You sign

in my book and I'll have Ms.—uh—Bennett witness it and
sign, too. Then I'll get Sergeant Franciotti to sign later.''

Mitchell went to a round table that stood beside an arm-
chair. The surface was covered with a mass of framed black-
and-white photos dating way back. Some were that sepia
tone you see in old pictures sometimes. He picked one up
and stared at it, then another, then another. His head was
shaking slowly as though something incomprehensible had
happened to him.

"This isn't my mother," he said. "This isn't Nina. This
isn't New York. Who the hell are these people?''

I walked over and looked at the photos he was holding.
The woman was young and wearing an out-of-date dress and
a hat. "I assumed—'' I started to say.

He turned the oval frame over, opened the clasps on the
back, and pulled out the photo of the woman. In a very
European hand, the kind of writing Nathan used, was written: "Renata, Leipzig, 1933.'' He put the photo and frame
down and opened a frame with a picture of a boy and girl.
The same handwriting labeled it, "Heinz, 4 Jahre, Karolla,
2 Jahre, 1939.''

"I don't believe this," Mitchell said. He walked to another table, scanned the pictures there, picked one up, and
looked at it closely. The man in it was a young Nathan,
bespectacled, in a double-breasted suit. Beside him was the
young woman of the other pictures. She was wearing a suit,
a hat, and a fur piece over her shoulders. The head of one
little mink could be clearly seen fastened to another piece of
fur. In her hands she held a small bouquet of white flowers.
If anything looked like a wedding picture, that did. Mitchell
turned it over. It was dated March 10, 1933. "He had another
family," Mitchell said, his voice ringing with misery. "He
had a wife and two children that he never told us about.''

"They must have died during the war," I said.

"But to keep it a secret. To drag out these pictures when
I was no longer welcome in his home— How the hell did he
get them through the war anyway? And my mother. There
isn't a single picture of her here. It's as if we were the ones

that died and they were the ones that lived." He looked dangerously pale.

"Come sit in the kitchen, and I'll give you a glass of water."

"I need something stronger than that." He followed me into the kitchen. "Over the refrigerator. There should be something there."

There was—several bottles of whiskey. I took one down and poured some into a glass. Mitchell drank it in two gulps. As he sat at the old table where Nathan and I had spent many pleasant hours talking, his color returned. "He had two separate lives," he said reflectively, "a good one and a bad one. And I was part of the bad one."

"Don't look at it that way. There was a war, and there was a time before and a time after."

"What my mother had to live through," he went on. "That bastard. That damned bastard. He treated her like dirt when she was alive, and he threw her memory away when she was dead."

"Do you want to look for pictures of your mother? They might be put away in a closet."

"Not now. I don't think I can take any more of my father right now. I'll have to come back anyway when they open up the apartment. I don't think Nina wants to set foot in here. My wife and I'll have to take care of it. Let's go."

Office Schuyler was standing just outside the doorway to the kitchen. "Had enough?" he asked.

"I think we're ready to go," I said. "Tell me, Officer, this Ramirez, how would he have gotten in?"

"Not too hard. He could've hid in one of the apartments on the floor and waited for the victim to come home."

"But the door is locked downstairs."

Schuyler smiled at my naïveté. "You wanna get in, you get in. Jesus coulda got the key from the landlord. You can be sure he didn't do this on his own."

We walked back to the door and waited while Schuyler locked it and, after filling in all the lines and captions, retaped it with fresh tape. As we went down the hall to the stairs, Mitchell shivered, although it wasn't particularly cold. At the stairwell I told him I would meet him downstairs in a little while, and I went up to tell Mrs. Paterno where the funeral was. Then I went down and did the same for Gallagher.

When I reached the ground floor, I saw Mitchell Herskovitz through the window in the door. He was looking down the street toward Riverside Park as though wondering how all of this had come to pass.

6

Mitchell and I arrived at the funeral home at one-thirty, half an hour before the funeral was due to start.

"You'd better wear one of these," he said, taking a black lacy circle from the top of a pile and handing it to me. "To cover your head," he explained.

I found a dish of hat pins and fastened the veil to my hair.

"And please sign the book. I want the family to know you were here."

Someone named Hillel Greenspan with an address on Riverside Drive had signed the first line. After I filled in my name and address, I joined Mitchell in a comfortable lounge room with sofas and chairs. An old man was sitting on one of the sofas, his cane held upright between his legs, talking to Mitchell. During lunch, Mitchell had recovered sufficiently that he felt able to put aside what he had learned that morning about his father and converse with the mourners. He told me that he still felt numb and he didn't look forward to enlightening his sister later that day, but he would get through this.

"I'd like you to meet Mr. Greenspan," he said as I walked into the room. "Mr. Greenspan helped my parents find the apartment when we first came to New York."

We shook hands, and I listened as Mr. Greenspan told us both what a wonderful person Nathan Herskovitz had been. Mitchell had just finished agreeing with one particular point when he looked toward the door and excused himself. A rather handsome couple had just come in, and Mitchell kissed the woman and shook hands heartily with the man. I assumed they were Nina and Gordon Passman. I told Mr. Greenspan I would be back soon, and I stood and took a few steps in their direction. Mitchell brought the couple over and introduced us.

"I apologize for my behavior on the phone the other day," Nina said as the men moved away to talk. "Mitchell said he explained."

"He did, and it's all right."

"I understand you've been very helpful to my father. I'm grateful to you for that. I wasn't able to help him myself. What I've learned as my father's daughter is that time doesn't heal all wounds. In some cases, it makes them worse."

"It's possible your father was sorry for what happened between you. He was very anxious to attend Yom Kippur services. I was going to take him there."

"My father repent?" She laughed, a jarring, brittle sound in the quiet room. "He'd have to go to a year of Yom Kippur services to repent for everything he did. I'm sorry. I promised myself I'd behave this afternoon. By the way, how did you find my phone number the other day?"

"It was on the flap of an envelope with your name and address printed on it. Your father kept it in the back of his address book."

A small smile played on her lips. "I wrote that letter a month after we were married, when my stationery was new and I was so happy to be Mrs. Gordon Passman. I told my father that I loved him, that I wanted us to remain a family, that we should meet and discuss our differences. He never responded. I wonder if he ever read the letter. Maybe he just tore off the flap so there'd be someone to notify if he ever ended up dead."

"He must have read it. He wrote your telephone number on the flap."

The little smile came back. "That's right. It makes it worse, doesn't it? He read it and rejected my offer. Well, it left him without a daughter, without grandchildren."

That troubled me, but it was none of my business. Several old people had come in while we were talking, and I noticed

Gallagher and Mrs. Paterno among them. I excused myself and went to say hello to them.

"Have you thought about leaving the building?" I asked Mrs. Paterno.

"That's all I think about, but I have nowhere to go."

"Do you know any of these people?" I asked both of them.

"I see them on the bench sometimes on Broadway," Gallagher said. "That fellow over there, he and Nathan were old pals." He indicated a tall, rather solid-looking man who had entered with a woman.

"That one I see sometimes in the supermarket," Mrs. Paterno said, looking at little Mr. Greenspan, who was just then lifting himself to his feet with the aid of his cane.

I realized people were moving toward another room, and we joined the small crowd. It was the first Jewish funeral I had ever attended, and it surprised me in many ways. The coffin was a shock. It was a very plain, unadorned box of a simple wood with a perfectly flat top. I guess we Catholics go in for more elaborate caskets, but the sight of that one gave me a chill.

My second surprise was the funeral service itself. It lasted exactly seven minutes, including a brief eulogy and what I took to be a prayer for the dead at the end. Then we left for the cemetery.

Mitchell had ordered a second limousine for Gallagher, Paterno, and me, although I told him I was quite able to drive. It was a long trip to the cemetery, and a fairly quiet one. After we talked about the Ramirez arrest, we were silent. At the burial, I saw Mrs. Paterno wipe away a tear, and Ian Gallagher looked desolate. I watched the simple coffin being lowered into the ground, and then Mitchell shoveled some earth over it. Nathan Herskovitz was gone.

As we returned to the limousines, Mitchell asked me to stay in the city and have dinner with him. That surprised me because I had expected him to spend the evening with his sister. I accepted, and after Gallagher and Mrs. Paterno were dropped off at home, I continued on to the funeral home, where the Herskovitz car was just arriving. Mitchell picked up the book with the signatures of the mourners, and I went to find a telephone. It was close to six, but I thought I might still be able to reach Arnold Gold at his office. I was right.

"You go to the funeral?" he asked when I told him who was calling.

"We just got back. There were a fair number of people at the funeral, but none of them went out to the cemetery except our inner circle."

"How're they holding up?"

"Pretty well. I think they're relieved there's been an arrest. Jack called me this morning and said they'd arrested a man named Ramirez."

"Typical dumb NYPD collar," Arnold said in his usual forthright manner. His sentiments about the police department are not exactly laudatory.

"You think he may not have done it?"

"I'm *sure* he didn't do it. I went over and talked to him this afternoon."

"You talked to Ramirez?" I was starting not to like this.

"I'm going to defend him, Chrissie. Every so often the cops do something so unforgivably stupid, I lose my cool, and this is one of them. You got a murder, you round up all the usual suspects and pick one to pin it on. I don't think they can even place him in the area at the time of the crime."

"Arnold, how can you defend him if you've been in court against Metropolitan Properties?"

"Who said anything about Metropolitan? Nobody's made a connection there. They've just arrested Ramirez. Damned sloppy investigative work. Franciotti probably needed one more arrest to make lieutenant."

"If Ramirez didn't do it, who do you think did?"

"Who the hell knows? Doesn't look like robbery. Maybe Herskovitz had an enemy."

"Maybe he did," I said. Maybe, indeed, he did.

Mitchell was as troubled as I at Arnold Gold's news that he was defending Ramirez. "That means it's not over," he said as we sat at dinner that evening. "I wonder when they'll let me in to clean up the apartment." He had told me earlier that he was leaving for Atlanta the next morning and would not return until the police gave him permission to go in.

"Arnold may be wrong. He's often more concerned with people's civil rights than with what actually happened. Ramirez may have done it. And the fact that someone's defending the suspect doesn't mean the police will change their minds. They've arrested the person they think is guilty. I expect they'll free up the apartment pretty soon, regardless of Arnold."

"I hope so."

"I know it's difficult to talk about, but you were pretty shocked by those pictures."

"Shocked beyond anything I can express in words. When I heard that he was dead, when you called me and afterward, when I talked to the police, I decided to put everything aside, all the animosity. I knew Nina was beyond forgiving him, but I wasn't. There would be a funeral, I would meet his old friends, bury him next to my mother. When I saw those pictures . . ." He shook his head. "Old friends must have come to visit him and seen them. How could he explain it?"

"It seems so odd that he never talked about that first family. What happened to him must have happened to many people. A family was wiped out, and the survivor started over. There's nothing shameful about it."

"Maybe there was something shameful about it."

I didn't know what he meant, and he didn't elaborate. "Mitchell, I think there's a good chance Ramirez did it, and if he did, he probably did it for Metropolitan Properties. Whether I like it or not, these things happen, and whatever Arnold feels about the police, they do a pretty good job. On the other hand, Arnold could be right about Ramirez, and someone else may have killed your father."

"I understand."

You have to start somewhere. When someone is killed in an apartment house, the police knock on every door, question people in every apartment, looking for clues, reasons.

In this case, they had accomplished all that on Saturday morning. I am not a professional anything, but I had done a bit of successful investigating a few months earlier, and I had a sense of where to start.

"Would you mind if I copied down the names in the guest book from this afternoon?" I asked Mitchell. "I'd just like to ask a few questions and see if I come up with anything."

"Not at all. I have it right here." He pulled it out of an attaché case he was carrying with him and gave it to me.

I spent the next few minutes copying names and addresses. They covered slightly more than a page of the guest book, and three of them were Gallagher, Paterno, and I. I returned the book, and he slid it into his case.

"I was kind of surprised when you asked me to join you this evening," I said. "I thought you'd spend some time with your sister."

Mitchell smiled. "It may not sound very good, but Nina and Gordon had theater tickets for tonight. They left for an early dinner when we got back to the funeral home."

"Do you think she would talk to me?" I asked.

"Probably. My sister's a good person. Don't let her relationship with our father get you off on the wrong foot. He was the anomaly in our lives."

I was starting to wonder. When people tell me something, I tend to believe them. On further reflection, I sometimes revise my opinion. I had known Nathan for nearly two months, and he had seemed a kind man caught in the collective problems of old age and modern real estate. Was it possible that he was the victim of a daughter who clearly despised him, of a wife who might not be the saint her children portrayed her to be, even of a son whose story might be open to some scrutiny? I had liked Nathan. Gallagher liked Nathan. Mrs. Paterno—well, Mrs. Paterno might not like anyone except herself, but perhaps I felt that way because I didn't really know her. There were enough questions floating in my head to justify my spending time finding answers.

"How old was your father?" I asked.

"Eighty-five on his last birthday. He was born in 1905."

"That surprises me. I took him for eighty. He was in very good condition."

"He was. He walked a lot when his legs were better. Even now, Mr. Gallagher said they often walked up to Broadway and sat in the sun. He never wanted to be a recluse, and he never became one."

We had come to the end of dinner, and I wanted to get home as soon as possible. My Tuesday class met at nine in the morning, and I needed my sleep. "Let me know when you come back to clean out the apartment. I'll be glad to help if you need another pair of hands."

"I'll do that."

He thanked me, paid the bill, and I drove him back to his hotel. I thought he drooped a little as he crossed the sidewalk and went through the door. It takes something out of you to spend a day as he had spent his, seeing that apartment first off and then burying his father. For all the problems in the Herskovitzes' lives, there had been affection between Mitchell and his father, maybe even love. It was more than I could say for Nina.

7

Melanie Gross is a wonderful neighbor. She has a sixth sense about me, which I appreciate. Just when I think I can't cook one more tasteless meal and eat it alone, she invites me for the kind of dinner you can only make for two or more people. When I thank her, I wonder if she understands how much I appreciate her hospitality.

Tuesday morning I ran into her on my morning jaunt. She was in her red sweat suit—I don't own one; I go out in plain old clothes—so she looked a little like Santa. Melanie is slightly on the plump side and very affable. We hadn't seen each other since before Yom Kippur, so we greeted each other like long-lost pals.

"He's everything you promised," I called, knowing she would understand I meant her cousin, Mark Brownstein.

"So how was it?"

"Very enjoyable."

"Think you'll see him again?"

"Probably." I had his prayer book, and he had said he'd retrieve it next time we saw each other.

"That's fabulous," Melanie said. She looked as happy as though it were happening to her.

We continued around the corner, talking and jogging. When I meet Melanie, I move faster. All I want in the morning is a brisk walk, but Mel wants speed and distance. We have learned to compromise. Perhaps that's why we've become friends.

She left me at my driveway and kept going. I got ready for

my day, breakfasted, gathered my papers, and left for my class.

I taught a group of sophomores and juniors who considered themselves contemporary women, often aggressively so. In the few short weeks that the semester had run, I had been surprised several times by the intensity of some students' wrath at what they characterized as "chauvinistic drivel" and "demeaning sentiments masquerading as poetry." It wasn't very much like teaching at St. Stephen's College. I had wondered, not aloud in class but to myself afterward, whether time and experience would temper their sentiments and their tongues, even as they sharpened mine. It must be wonderful to be eighteen or nineteen and to be *so sure*. It's something I missed.

The class lasted two and a half hours, which was rough going, but it was my only fixed commitment each week. We took a brief break after ninety minutes; then I didn't feel guilty if I went over a few minutes at the end. That morning a student from whom I'd heard almost nothing suddenly came alive. She challenged the "chauvinistic drivel" proponent, saying human emotions other than anger and resentment had a legitimate place in literature, that love of the opposite sex did not necessarily imply relinquishing one's rights. She was angry and articulate. I wondered whether she had fallen in love over the weekend or simply begun to read the assigned poems. I was glad to hear from her.

I stopped for a sandwich at the cafeteria and then drove into New York, voices from my class still ringing in my ears. I wanted to get started asking questions about Nathan Herskovitz, and I thought the best place to start was with the other tenants. As I rolled slowly down Broadway looking for a free meter, I spotted Gallagher on a bench.

Broadway is a funny street. North of Columbus Circle an unkempt median of scraggly grass and weeds divides the north- and southbound lanes. At intersections there are old wooden park benches facing north at one end and south at the other. The benches are chipped and cracked by age, weather, and use, and they bear small pieces of often painful history in engraved remembrances. On sunny afternoons they are usually occupied, mostly by old people of a variety of races and ethnic origins. Some sit in silence, some talk to themselves, still others regale fellow bench sitters. Gallagher was sitting next to a black woman who must have been half his age. On the other side of her was an old white woman with a newspaper in her lap, perhaps to keep her warm as she was raising her face toward the sun. A small van pulled out of a parking spot just ahead of me, and I swerved in without even signaling. An hour had been granted me.

I got out and walked back to where Gallagher sat between the two women. "Hello, Ian," I called as I crossed to the divider.

His face lit up. "Well, darlin', it's good to see you." He stood and clasped my hand in his.

"How 'bout a cup of coffee?" I offered.

"Good idea."

We crossed to the other side of Broadway and went into a coffee shop. Once ensconced in a booth, I suggested that Ian try the tuna sandwich with melted cheese. These old people have a nasty habit of eating tea and toast meal after meal, and sometimes, when they're not hungry (they tell me), tea and toast minus the toast. I try to get some protein in them, and a few calories as well. Ian obliged, which meant to me he hadn't had much, if anything, for lunch.

"Ian," I said when I'd given the order, "Arnold Gold thinks Ramirez may not have done it." I didn't want to use the word "murder," and I didn't need to.

"Then who did?"

"He has no idea. I know you think Metropolitan Properties is involved, but it's possible they're not. It's possible someone wanted to kill Nathan because he was Nathan."

"What are you tellin' me?"

"I want to find out as much as I can about Nathan. Maybe something will turn up."

"Don't ask me. If Herskovitz had secrets, they died with him. We only talked about the weather and the landlord."

"He told you where to find his address book," I said, ignoring his disclaimer.

"True, true. You think about those things when you get to our age."

"When did you move into 603?" I asked.

"Thirty-nine. Had a new wife and a new job. I worked for the city then. Drove a trolley car."

"Were you in the war?"

"Couldn't keep me out." He smiled at the memory.

"Did you join up then?"

"Wanted to, but they drafted me first. Covered the whole Pacific before it was over—Hawaii, Guam, Okinawa. I was out in Guam when my son was born."

"And then you came back to the same apartment and the same job?"

"Same kinda job, I drove a bus. Nice pension, good vacation. Retired at sixty-five. Fifteen years already. Seems like yesterday."

From the distant look in his eyes, I guessed he was seeing it all again. When he resumed eating, I asked, "When did you first meet Nathan?"

"Hard to say. You run into people in the lobby, you say hello, talk about the weather, that kinda thing. When Metropolitan took over, that's when we all started to look each other in the eye and think of people as neighbors. That was three, four years ago. Some folks up and left right at the beginning. They got a nice little bonus for going, and they found another place, and that was the end of 'em. Most of us stayed and worried. Finally we had a tenants' meeting, that was a long time ago, and hired on a lawyer to see if he could fix it so we could stay. It bought us a little time is all. Then things stopped working. The elevator was off more 'n it was on. Light bulbs in the halls disappeared. Strange things went on in the empty apartments, a fire here, a fire there. Every month someone else moved out. When they turned off the electricity, that's when the rest of 'em deserted. One day there was just the three of us."

"That was last year," I said.

"Round about Christmas. The sweethearts thought they'd get us out by year's end."

"But you must have known Nathan before then."

"Well, we'd been sittin' on benches for a year or two," he said with typical understatement.

"And grousing about the weather and the landlord."

"And grousin', yes. Sounds about right, darlin'."

"Did you ever know the rest of his family?"

"Probably ran into 'em in the lobby from time to time, but I never knew one from another."

"You didn't know his wife."

"Wouldn't recognize her if I fell over her."

"Did you ever go to Nathan's apartment?"

"Not once."

That surprised me. "With just the three of you alone in that big building, you never went up to visit him?"

"Too far up," Gallagher said. "He was on five. He came to me. We'd be comin' back from Broadway and hoistin' ourselves up those stairs and I'd say, 'Herskovitz, stop in and rest a minute,' and he'd say, 'Good idea.' I was halfway between the lobby and his place, good for stoppin' over."

"Did you ever eat together?"

"Nah. We ate all different. He took his tea this way, I took mine that way. You can't eat outside the family, darlin'. You should know that."

I started to understand how difficult it might be to form cross-cultural friendships among these old people so set in their ways. "Ian, a lot of people came to his funeral. Did he visit with people? Did he have friends?"

"Oh, sure he did. I saw him take a taxi sometimes when he got an invite to dinner."

"Did he have enemies?" I had taken my time getting around to it, but I was glad, because now it paid off.

"Every man has enemies," Gallagher said in a low voice.

"Tell me about Nathan's."

He had finished his sandwich and was sipping a cup of hot chocolate to which he had added some cream. "There was something." He sipped the chocolate again.

"It could be important, Ian."

He shrugged. "He didn't say much."

"Tell me what he did say."

"It was a phone call now and again. He'd sit down on the bench and mumble something."

"What kind of something?"

"That they were bothering him. He called them something in another language. Herskovitz did that when he was sore."

"Ian, if you think of anything else, I'll be around."

"Well, I hope so. What would we do without you?"

We stopped at the supermarket and picked up a few necessities. Ian ate a lot of TV-type dinners. Sometimes when I saw the price of them, I thought how much better off he would be to cook up a stew with fresh meat and vegetables on his own stove. Surely he had the time. There was a weird irony in the similarity between the eating habits of Ian Gallagher and those of Mark Brownstein, one at the bottom of the economic scale, one at the top. Gallagher used his oven to heat up his TV dinners, and Mark popped gourmet frozen meals into his microwave, but the net result was probably pretty much the same.

On the way back to 603, I dropped another quarter into the parking meter. When we got to the third floor, having taken the stairs slowly for Ian's sake, I remembered the keys Nathan had given me.

"Nathan had the keys to your apartment, didn't he?" I asked.

"That was the arrangement."

"Had he ever used them?"

"Not unless he sneaked in when I wasn't there."

"I think he gave me the keys to your place by accident last week." I pulled them out of my bag. "Mind if I give them a try?"

"Anything you fancy."

I tried the Segal first. It wouldn't even go in.

"Can't be my keys," Gallagher said. "I got three." He

took his out and used them, pushing the door open after turning the last one.

"He must have made it for me and forgotten to try it first." I dropped it back in my bag, feeling irritated that some local hardware store had ripped him off.

I helped Ian put the groceries away and said I'd see him soon. Instead of going down, I went up to five to try the key once more. Maybe it had been my fault that a new key had failed to work properly.

But try as I might, I couldn't get the key to turn in the lock. In a way, I was glad. I didn't want to relive the horror of walking into that living room on Saturday morning.

I went back to the stairwell and opened the door. Although I've tried not to dwell on that stairwell, I can tell you that every time I entered it, it was with misgivings, and every time I left it, it was with relief. This time, as the door closed heavily behind me, I was aware of a sound. It was like a drummer tapping rapidly with his sticks on some surface, probably the cinder block wall of the stairwell. I stopped, feeling more than my usual amount of anxiety.

The noise stopped as suddenly as it had begun, and I heard footsteps. "Mrs. Paterno?" I called.

There was no answer, not that I expected one. The sound had come from above, and she was the only legitimate occupant of the sixth floor. Above that, of course, was the roof. I suppose if I'd been a hotshot, gun-toting detective, I would have bounded up the stairs, looking for whatever trouble was up there.

But I was an unarmed female who'd never been trained in the martial arts, and I really wanted to live to see tomorrow. I started down the stairs, and the tapping began again. I moved faster. The tapping stopped, and heavy footsteps descended. Whoever it was was after me.

I knew I could detour at any floor, but what would be the purpose? Four was completely empty—or should be. The locks on all the empty apartments had been removed, and the best I could do was try to hide behind a door in one while my pursuer looked behind the doors in another. And if he had some sort of a weapon, which was likely if he was an intruder, I'd lose in the end anyway. Big.

By the time I decided to keep going, I had passed three, where Gallagher might have been my salvation, so I kept on, praying that I wouldn't trip on a stair tread and kill myself before the guy upstairs got his chance.

I reached the door to the lobby and threw myself into it, panting. But it was too soon to stop. I ran out the inner door and then the outer one, and then, at a slower run, up the street. The anonymity of a New York street has its advantages. A woman was wheeling a baby carriage. I passed her. Across the street some children carrying schoolbags were giggling together. I went over to their side and finally looked back. There were no men on the street, no one at all who looked threatening. I slowed down. I breathed deeply. I got to Broadway and found my car.

I don't remember exactly where I was when I got the uncomfortable feeling that I was being tailed. I was on one of the highways leading to Oakwood with cars fore and aft, left and right. I told myself I was getting paranoid, but the feeling persisted. From time to time I would glance in the rearview mirror, but it seemed there was a different car there each time. Still there was that feeling.

When traffic thinned out some, I checked more frequently. An old tan falling-apart something-or-other was behind me. You know that company that says they rent wrecks? This was one they would give away. There was a man at the wheel, but he was too far back for me to get much of an impression of his looks.

I turned off for Oakwood without signaling and saw him follow. He lagged behind as I stopped for a light at the end of the exit ramp, but he speeded up to make the green.

This isn't happening to me, I told myself. But it was. I couldn't drive home and let him know where I lived. One nice thing about a small town is that the police are always friendly. When I got into Oakwood, I drove to the police station. They have a big parking lot at the rear of the building, and it's always nearly empty. I pulled into the space nearest the building and got out. As I walked to the door, the old, beat-up car glided by without stopping. I went inside. If they hurried, they might pick him up on his way back to the highway.

I had every intention of reporting to the police what had happened. That is, until I saw who was on duty. Oakwood had hired a new policeman last summer, twenty-two years old and cherubic. I am not without pride, sinful as that may once have sounded. I just couldn't bring myself to tell that adorable child in a blue uniform what had happened.

He looked up and smiled.

"I—uh—I think I left something on the stove," I said, flustered.

"See you later," he called.

Not over my dead body.

I went out to my car. It was still the only one in the lot. I walked to the curb and looked up and down the quiet residential street. Nothing. I went back to my car and drove in and out of streets until I was satisfied the wreck was gone. Then I went home.

That evening I called Nina Passman. It was the first time I had spoken to her since her brother had told her about the pictures in Nathan's living room. She seemed reluctant to talk to me, and then, quite suddenly, changed.

"I have to be in the city tomorrow. Could we meet at two?"

"Two's fine."

"Gordon and I have a little pied-à-terre in Manhattan." She gave me the address. "Apartment 17C. I'll see you then."

I suppressed a giggle as I hung up. A pied-à-terre, "foot on earth," an apartment in the sky, a place the Passmans could stay at after the theater or a tiring day, when driving thirty miles was just too much for them or taking the Long Island Railroad was more than they could bear. Well, at least she would talk to me.

8

I started my day on Wednesday by calling the first name in the book from the funeral home, Hillel Greenspan. He said, sure, sure, I could come and talk to him whenever I got there. It was all the encouragement I needed.

New York is a city with alternate-side-of-the-street parking rules that theoretically provide time for street cleaning and generate some much-needed revenue, but in reality they are designed to drive people crazy. On one side of the street you can't park from 8:00 A.M. to 11:00 A.M. on Mondays, Wednesdays, and Fridays. On the other side you can't park during those hours on Tuesdays, Thursdays, and Saturdays. On some streets the hours are eleven to two, and sometimes the restrictions are two days a week instead of three. And in areas where the buildings are old, like the West Side of Manhattan, there are virtually no places to park except for the street. Buildings erected before the Second World War never provided off-street parking, probably because no one could imagine so many people owning so many cars. Sometimes I can't quite imagine it myself.

So finding a spot is a game. What many people do is simply double-park on today's "good side" for the three street-cleaning hours and then rush to get a spot that's good the next day. It's a lifelong battle. And if you have a good spot today and you want to take your car out only to find a solid line of cars double-parked next to you, there's virtually nothing you can do. In most cases, the police won't even ticket the double-parker. If they do, the ticket adds to the litter.

What I do is try to arrive half an hour before the parking restrictions end so that I can park on either side (since I won't be staying overnight) during the half hour when everyone rushes for cover. Or I look for a meter on Broadway, which means I have an hour before I have to run back and drop in more quarter.

On that Wednesday morning, luck was with me. Someone actually pulled out of a good space as I coasted down Riverside Drive. It was a small car, but that's what I drive, and I backed in easily. If you believe in good omens, that surely signaled an auspicious start to the day.

Hillel Greenspan's apartment had large rooms overlooking the Hudson River in the Seventies. From the eighth floor the view was beautiful. The strip of green that was Riverside Park stretched as far as you could see to the right and a few blocks to the left across the street, right down to the river. The river itself is quite magnificent, and the George Washington Bridge off to the right was spectacular.

I saw all this from the windows of his living room.

"You like the view?" he asked from his chair where he could probably see no more than the sky.

"It's beautiful. Have you lived here long?"

"Forever." He smiled.

"That's a long time. Mitchell told me you helped Nathan find his apartment."

"I did, I did. I knew someone who was moving. We paid a little here, a little there, we got the apartment for the Herskovitzes."

"How did you know him, Mr. Greenspan?"

"How do you know people?" he asked back. "You grow up with them, you work with them."

"You knew him in Europe, then, before the war."

"Exactly."

Hillel Greenspan spoke English fluently with the smallest of accents, much as Nathan had. Until Mitchell had told me otherwise, I had assumed that Nathan had come to New York as a young man, long before the war. Knowing how old he was when he immigrated, I appreciated how well he spoke the language.

"What did Nathan do in Europe?"

"In Europe he was a lawyer."

"Nathan was a lawyer? He told me he'd been in business."

"Here he was in business, there he was a lawyer. Law doesn't move around so easy. If you're an accountant, the numbers stay the same. Laws are different. He came here, he had to work. He worked."

"What did he do?"

"He sold blankets."

I felt a small pang of what might have been Nathan's pain. This was what the war had done, taken a man educated in the law, a respected professional, and turned him into a small businessman.

"A beautiful store," Mr. Greenspan said, filling the silence. "Blankets, quilts, pillows, quality goods."

"Did his wife work in the store with him?"

He eyed me curiously before he answered. "His wife? No. She had little children. She stayed home."

"She died a long time ago, didn't she?"

"Could be thirty years already. Maybe longer."

"Was she sick?"

Mr. Greenspan pursed his lips. Then he nodded his head. "From the very beginning," he said. "The war made a lot of people sick."

"Did you know her?"

"Sure I knew her. We were all friends."

"When did you come to this country, Mr. Greenspan?"

"You see," he said, "there are two kinds of people. There are those that have luck and those that need luck. Or you could say there are those that think of themselves and those that think of others. Or you could look at it this way: There are people who do what is required of them and people who can never do enough."

I wondered where this was leading. It had been a simple question. I had expected a short answer.

"You wonder why I answer your question this way."

"I'm sure you have a good reason," I said with a smile.

"What I am telling you is that I was the man with the luck, I was the man who thought of myself, I was the man who did what was required. I came to this country in 1939. Nathan could have come. But Nathan was a man who could never give up. He stayed. If he stayed one day more, he saved another person, maybe another family. One day becomes two, two becomes three, and pretty soon he finds himself in a camp, his family torn apart, his whole life reduced to a number on his arm. And I, the man with luck, find myself on Riverside Drive, where every night I see the sun set and I know I have lived another day."

"You're saying that Nathan stayed on in Europe to help other people get out."

"Exactly. He had friends, connections, clients, people who owed him something. He used it. He used everything. In the whole world, there wasn't a better man than Nathan Herskovitz."

For the first time since Sunday, I felt there was someone else in the world who had liked and respected Nathan. "I'm glad to hear you say that, Mr. Greenspan. I knew him only a couple of months, but I thought he was a fine man."

"I'm not surprised to hear it. He said nice things about you, too."

"Is it possible that he had any enemies?"

"Everyone has enemies. A man who collects what is owed him can be hated."

"But those were people in Europe."

"Some came here."

His words gave me a chill. "Is there someone who might have wanted to kill him?"

The old man smiled. "It's too late for that now, don't you think so? You kill an old man because he has money, or because he lives in an apartment you want for yourself, not because he collected a debt fifty years ago. You think someone from Nathan's past beat him to death?"

"I don't know."

"Such things don't happen."

I decided to say what I was thinking. "I think Nathan was sorry for something he did."

"We're all sorry," the little man in the big chair said. "All of us. You get old, you get sorry. We don't get killed for it."

"Would you mind if I came back to ask you some more questions?" I asked.

"Sure, come. Come at five o'clock and see the sun go down. Already I've seen more than eighteen thousand sunsets from my window. God willing, I could live to see twenty. Just call before you come. I'm a busy man. Lately I go to a lot of funerals."

I had a few hours till my appointment with Nina Passman. Since my parking space was good all day, I decided to leave the car and take the crosstown bus that goes along Seventy-ninth Street and then through Central Park. If I got off at Park Avenue, I would have only a few blocks to walk, and somewhere in between, I could have lunch.

I took the bus another stop to Lexington Avenue, which gave me more choices for lunch. After I had eaten in a nice little coffee shop, I tried Arnold Gold from a pay phone. He was there.

"Give me the picture," he said when he got on the phone. "Are you trying to prove me right or wrong?"

"I know better than to try to prove you wrong, Arnold. I'm just looking for truth with a capital T."

"Good luck. I've been looking all my life."

"Did you get the autopsy report on Nathan yet?"

"This very day. He was killed late Friday afternoon or early evening. If they'd just waited awhile, he would have died of natural causes. His arteries were blocked, and it looks like he had a tumor that probably would have gotten him before next Yom Kippur."

Inscribe me for blessing in the Book of Life.

"Do they know what killed him?"

"Sure. Multiple blows to the head with a hard object, hard

enough to dent his skull. Nothing like it was found in the apartment.''

''So the killer took it with him.''

''Looks that way. Did you notice anything missing?''

''No, but I'll give it some thought. I wasn't in there very long.''

''Maybe Gallagher would know.''

''I talked to Gallagher yesterday. He was never in Nathan's apartment.''

''Strange old guys, those two. What about the woman?''

''She's so reclusive, I can't imagine she had anything to do with either of the men. The first time she let me in to her apartment was Saturday when I was looking for the key.''

''Well, Chrissie, someone got in and did a job on him, and we can't expect any help from the police. They think they've got their man, and that gives them a cleared case. Nice and easy for them.''

''Well, my case is just opening. For what it's worth, I'm talking to some people. I'll let you know what I find out.''

I did some window-shopping—you can hardly avoid it in that part of the city—then walked over to the Passmans' pied-à-terre. Having a foot on the ground on the seventeenth floor is really stretching a metaphor, I thought as I zoomed up-stairs in the elevator after being announced. But whatever you called it, it was a lovely place, parquet floors covered with a thick Chinese rug with a lot of blues, a small round marble table with two chairs in the eating area, and comfortable furniture for sitting near a wall of windows that looked east. If Mr. Greenspan saw the sun set from his living room, the Passmans could see it rise from theirs.

I thanked Nina Passman for seeing me and told her to call me Chris. She showed me to the sofa and asked me how I wanted my coffee, but she didn't reciprocate on the first-name offer.

''The lawyer representing the tenants in your father's building doesn't think the police have arrested the right man,'' I began while she was pouring coffee from a brightly colored flowered coffeepot that matched the cups and cake plates.

"Is that why you're talking to me?"

"There's an answer somewhere, and maybe it's in your father's life. I want to find out everything I can about him. If someone else killed him, it was probably someone who knew him. Nothing was stolen from the apartment."

"I haven't seen or spoken to my father in many years."

"But you wrote to him after you were married. You wanted to renew your relationship with him, didn't you?"

She looked thoughtful. I had already told her that only a scrap of the envelope remained. With the letter gone, she could concoct any story she wanted, and I wondered if her thoughtfulness was devoted to that.

"I wanted to talk to him," she said finally. "I wanted to meet with him and have him explain certain things. I thought it might be possible to pick up some kind of relationship with him. He never answered the letter."

"I don't suppose you want to tell me what those things were that you wanted to talk to him about."

"I don't want to talk about it with you or anyone else."

"This is wonderful coffee," I said, thinking I was wasting an afternoon.

"This is a great neighborhood to live in. You can buy coffee beans and spices and fine pastry. Every time we come here, even if it's just an overnight, it feels like a vacation."

"Nina," I said, presuming the right to call her by her first name, "were you well off when you were growing up?"

"We never wanted for anything, if that's what you mean. I have no idea how much my father earned. We had nice furniture, enough clothes, we went to good schools. It wasn't something I worried about."

"Who took care of you after your mother died?"

She paused again. That was it, of course, the mother. She knew now from her brother that there had been another family before the war, and it had made her sensitive.

"We took care of ourselves. I had an aunt and uncle up near Columbia who helped out sometimes, invited us to dinner, helped me buy special clothes, that kind of thing. But Mitchell and I managed on our own."

"When did she die?"

Another pause. "When I was ten—1959."

"Mitchell indicated she hadn't been well."

"Really?"

"He said he used to think it was the war, but maybe she was just sick. And I saw Mr. Greenspan this morning, and he told me she was sick."

She gave me one of those smiles that had nothing to do with pleasure. She was a tough lady who had adapted to a tough world she had not made for herself. I felt sorry for her, but I couldn't quite like her.

"Did he answer all your questions with questions and treat you to the philosophy of life à la Hillel Greenspan?"

"I guess he did, but I kind of enjoyed it. What I don't quite understand is how, if your mother was sick, she managed to take her children to concerts and walks in the park and all the things Mitchell remembers."

"My mother wasn't sick, Miss Bennett. My mother was abused by a man who didn't love her."

"Do you mean he hurt her?"

"Not physically. My father wasn't violent. He just ignored her. He lived inside himself. Life was a disappointment to him. His wife disappointed him, his children disappointed him. No one lived up to his expectations. So he was content to sit with his dreams. Of course, they weren't dreams. When Mitchell told me on Monday about the pictures, it all became clear. He sat with memories. The wife who was everything, the children who would have grown up to be stars. All we ever did was intrude on those dreams."

"Do you think your mother knew about his first family?"

"It's possible. Mitchell and I certainly didn't."

"How did she die, Nina?" I asked.

"How do you think she died? She killed herself."

I knew that was what she had been trying not to tell me. "I'm so sorry," I said.

"And if you want the rest of it, I'm the one who came

home from school and found her with her head in the oven and the whole apartment stinking of gas. A scared ten-year-old having to cope with that. And then . . .''

I waited while she decided whether or not to go on.

''My father didn't go to the funeral,'' she said finally. ''He told us he was too upset.''

''Maybe he was.'' I had read that Mary Todd Lincoln had been too distraught to attend Lincoln's funeral, and the thought of that touched me.

''Anything is possible.'' She sat back against the cushions for the first time, no longer able to hold her back properly erect.

I found this new Nina easier to like than the old perfectionist who had seemed to be playing a part. Suddenly I could see that little ten-year-old in her face, the one who had opened the door and smelled the gas, who had run into the kitchen and seen what was left of her mother.

''Well, you know it all now,'' she said. ''I don't know what you'll do with it. It isn't likely to help find my father's killer.''

''Is that what you wrote to him about after you were married? That you wanted to talk to him about your mother's death?''

''I wanted reasons from him. I wanted explanations. I wanted to hear him say, 'I hurt your mother and I'm sorry for it.' But my father wasn't the kind of person who could say that. He was never sorry for anything. By the time I was married, we could hardly look at each other. And I suppose Mitchell told you about their falling-out.''

''He did.''

''So that left him with nothing, no children, no grandchildren. What did he do with himself?''

''He spent a lot of time alone in that apartment, perhaps with his memories.''

''Was there anything else you wanted?'' She had transformed herself back into the perfect matron, and I understood it was time to go.

"You've been very generous," I said, standing. "I appreciate it."

We said our good-byes and I went down the carpeted, lighted hall to the swift, silent elevator that worked without a hitch and kept me under surveillance with a camera over my head.

I had gotten more than I had bargained for.

9

I took the crosstown bus back to the West Side. My car
was still where I'd left it, apparently intact. In New York that
often ranks as a happy surprise. When I first saw them, I was
amused at the signs, in English and Spanish, hand-lettered
and professionally printed, proclaiming that there was "no
radio" in car after car parked on city streets. I no longer find
anything funny about them, but my car is so old and so cheap,
I can't quite believe anyone would think there was something
of value inside.

I was about to unlock the door when I changed my mind,
crossed the street to where the apartment houses formed an
impregnable wall, almost like the face of a cliff, across from
the park, and went back to Mr. Greenspan's address. I announced myself and was buzzed in. A hefty, middle-aged
woman in an apron opened the door for me. A smell of food
cooking in an unseen kitchen gave the apartment a warm,
homey atmosphere.

"You're too early for the sun," the little man in the chair
said as I entered the living room.

"I had another question."

"Make yourself comfortable."

I sat near the windows. "Did you know about Nathan's
first family in Europe?" I asked.

"Why would you want to know such a thing?"

"Because I think it may have something to do with his
death."

"Believe me, it didn't. And yes, sure I knew. I knew Re-

68

nata. I knew the babies. They were part of Nathan Hersko-vitz's first life.''

"Did the second Mrs. Herskovitz know about the first Mrs. Herskovitz?''

"You see, young lady, you look at it all wrong. When you say the first Mrs. Herskovitz and the second Mrs. Hersko-vitz, that's American, that's divorce. It wasn't like that for Nathan. Nathan had a first life and a second life. This, here—'' he jabbed his index finger toward the floor "—was his second life. Did Hannah know about the first life? Maybe. Probably. Maybe she had one, too. That's between husband and wife.''

"His children never knew until the day of his funeral. Mitchell walked into the apartment Monday morning and saw the pictures.''

"You want me to blame Nathan that his son didn't visit him more? If the son had visited, he would have known a long time ago what he just found out. Nathan needed com-pany in his old age. He didn't have his children, so he found it in his pictures.''

I thanked Mr. Greenspan and went down to my car. Driv-ing home, I wondered whether Nathan had found company earlier in his life, when Hannah was still alive, and with whom.

Jack called that evening and we had a nice, long talk. I told him about Mrs. Herskovitz's suicide.

"You asking for a file?''

"Not yet,'' I said. "I don't think it'll tell me anything I'll need. The daughter says Nathan neglected his wife to the point of abuse.''

"Happens.''

"I spent a lot of time talking to him, Jack. It's true he didn't ooze sweetness, but I didn't sense the kind of nastiness I hear from his family.''

"You're hearing one side. They have their gripes, but he may have had good reasons for what he did. Or he may have just been a mean bastard who drove his wife to suicide and his children out of his life. Is Gold pretty sure Ramirez didn't do it, or is he just playing the devil's advocate in all this?''

I frequently sensed an antagonism between these two men, who had never met but who had heard of each other through me. To Jack, Arnold was that lawyer type who hated cops and would rather free a hundred killers than let the system make one little mistake. To Arnold, Jack was my cop boyfriend who had to defend a corrupt system because he was part of it. I sensed, however, that Arnold tried to rein his feelings, knowing that I cared for Jack and respecting my ability to choose wisely.

''I think he's sure,'' I said. ''I don't think this is a legal quibble.''

''I hope you're right.''

''Jack,'' I said, feeling uncertain about what I was going to say, ''if I thought I was being followed, what would I do?''

When you say something like that to Jack, he's suddenly all business. ''You tell me about it and I come over and take care of the guy. What's going on?''

''I'm not sure.''

''You're looking into a homicide, Chris. If the owners of that building hired a guy to do a job and you find out something they don't want you to know, you're in for a pile of trouble.''

''Maybe it was my imagination.'' I'd seen Jack once before when my life was in danger, something I could live nicely without seeing again.

''You want to tell me?''

''It was just paranoia.''

''You call if you need help. And don't forget 911.''

''OK.''

''We on for Saturday?''

''Sure.''

''Let's make it early. I have to spend Sunday with my books.''

We set a time and said good night. I went to my study, took a sheet of paper, and wrote down a few things. First life, second life, first family, second family, Hannah commits suicide, Nina finds her, Nina hates Nathan for driving Hannah to suicide.

On another sheet I wrote different things: Nathan Herskovitz, lawyer, connections, calls in debts, waits too long to save himself and his family.

Then I wrote some questions: Did people pay him for saving them? (Where's the money?) Did he deny help to someone? To many people? To the wrong people? Was he involved in some kind of illicit trade?

I had no answers. The more time I spent thinking, the more questions I had. I left the desk with the sheets lying as I had left them, hoping for a flash of insight, of illumination, to lead me along the right trail. From where I stood, it looked pretty murky.

I went downstairs to check that the doors were locked and to turn off lights. The phone rang as I was leaving the kitchen. It was Mitchell Herskovitz. He had finally reached Sergeant Franciotti, who said the apartment would be available to him on Friday. He and his wife would not be able to come up this weekend, but they had paid a month's rent and would fly to New York next Friday night and start the job of cleaning up the apartment Saturday morning. If I wanted to drop by and say hello, I was welcome.

I said I would and I looked forward to seeing them next week.

Thursday morning I drove into the city and went to 603. I wanted to see whether the police were back today for a last look at Nathan's apartment. Before going into the stairwell, I took out my flashlight and psyched myself up, repeating what I had told Jack, that it was all paranoia, that I was too sensible and well adjusted to be affected by a little noise and a beat-up old car that may have had a legitimate reason to drive to Oakwood.

It didn't work very well. I pulled open the door and flashed the light around. It was perfectly quiet, and nothing was visible besides the stairs. I started up.

It was quiet all the way to five except for my pounding heart and the labored breathing that the climb always brought on. I stepped out into the hallway on five and stopped to listen. I have to tell you that it was never completely silent on those floors. If you walked into a vacant apartment, you could see armies of roaches that had taken up habitation. It's not the sort of thing I like to talk about, but that's what that building was like. Just walking through an empty apartment, you stepped on a few, and you could feel and hear it happen. I know because I ventured into one or two of those apartments once—and then never again.

And the roaches were the least of it. I knew the basement was a breeding ground for rats. Gallagher had said something once about a telephone installer coming up from the basement white as a sheet—and that had been in the good old days.

Anyway, the floor seemed empty of human beings, so I went down the hall to apartment D. The door was ajar, the crime scene tape cut neatly. I pushed the door, calling, "Hello. Anyone here?" as I went in. I figured the police were in there, doing whatever last-minute things they do before turning over the premises to the family.

But it was perfectly quiet inside, and I found myself getting angry that the police could have been so careless as to walk out without closing and locking the door. I passed the study, the master bedroom, the bathroom, the kitchen. All seemed just as I had last seen it on Monday morning.

I turned in to the living room, steeling myself, and got the shock of my life. From a point a foot or so above the floor to a couple of feet above that, a large hole had been gouged in the wall between the living room and the apartment next door, a hole easily large enough for a person to pass through. Someone had gained access to the building, gone into the abandoned, unlocked apartment that was a mirror image of this one, and drilled through the common wall. Whoever did it could have worked at a leisurely pace through the night. No one would have heard the noise except just possibly Mrs.

Paterno, who lived upstairs, but her apartment was at the other end of the building—and she minded her business.

I had no particular fear that the intruder was still in the apartment. He had left through the front door, probably hours ago. But just to make sure, I moved quietly from room to room.

The apartment was not tossed in the usual sense of having all the contents strewn around, furniture slashed, everything displaced. Instead, an effort had been made to leave things much as they had been, or perhaps the intruder had known exactly what he was looking for, and tossing had not been necessary.

Sofa cushions had been lifted and not put back precisely in place; bedding was somewhat awry; dresser drawers had been opened and not completely closed. I pulled open one drawer and saw that the contents had been pushed around—but, of course, I had no idea how neat Nathan had been.

Since closets seemed the likeliest place to keep valuables, I went around opening them and looking inside. They, too, showed a kind of mild disarray, but nothing pointing to a thorough search.

I tried to think why the killer would not have searched the apartment immediately after the murder. If he had wanted something from Nathan, that would have been the time to look for it. If he had found out later that Nathan had something of value, why kill him in the first place? It didn't make sense.

I knew I should be calling the police instead of looking around a crime scene, but it seemed an opportune time to go through the apartment without police or family observing me. Before starting, I went to the kitchen, where a pair of yellow rubber gloves hung over the side of a plastic bucket under the sink. Nathan had done whatever cleaning up he did while wearing them, and they would keep my fingerprints from being found on his possessions, assuming the police intended to dust the apartment or its contents a second time.

I started in the living room. Except for the bloodstains and the disfiguring hole in the wall, it looked exactly as I had seen it on the several occasions that I had visited the apartment. If something was missing, it certainly wasn't obvious. The kitchen, too, looked intact. The ever-present bottle of Lysol stood beside the sink, testimony to Nathan's belief that it would prevent almost anything contagious if squirted generously. The dishes were all stacked in the cabinets. One water glass with fingerprint powder still clinging to it stood on the drain board. There were stains and dust, but no fingerprints.

The bathroom was also in order. A second bottle of Lysol was on the floor under that sink. Toothbrushes and toothpaste lay in their usual places. The medicine chest was ajar, but I could not remember seeing it after the police were here, and it was always possible they had looked inside and not closed the mirrored door.

The master bedroom was in some disarray. The bed was no longer neatly made. Drawers were not flush. I pulled one drawer after another open and moved my hands around inside. I felt nothing but the softness of underwear, socks, and ties. All of Nathan's shirts were sent to be laundered, and now they lay in their plastic wrappings, folded around their cardboards, occupying one whole drawer. I closed it.

An old wind-up alarm clock stood on one night table, frozen at 4:37—A.M. or P.M., it didn't matter anymore for its owner. On his last day of life, Nathan had not wound it. In the drawer, held together with a rubber band, were many months' worth of bank statements. Nathan maintained a rather large balance in his checking account, more than twenty-three thousand dollars on the most recent statement. I had learned only in the last months how to handle a checking account myself, never having had any money at my disposal. I put the statements back and looked in the drawer in the other night table. There were several softcover books there, probably nocturnal reading. One, I noticed, was a collection of poetry that we had talked about early in September. I felt touched that he had bought it at my recommendation.

I pulled one of the cartons out of the closet. A cord fell

from it. It must have been tied before the police or the intruder had opened it. Inside, like the contents of a personal time capsule, were a lifetime's worth of photographs and snapshots. I looked in the top album. There were the pictures of Nathan's second family, his second life. A young woman held a baby, and a little boy, almost certainly Mitchell at about three, stood next to her, clutching her coat. Although the background was not very clear, I guessed it was Riverside Park.

I flipped through the pages, watching the children grow. Under the album was a group of *Playbill*s from long-ago plays, and under them, the kinds of awards children get in school. Mitchell had gotten a math prize; Nina had been awarded a poetry prize.

He could hardly have hated them, I thought, if he kept all these things.

A second carton had binders of papers, the kinds of things people hold on to so they'll have warranties if an appliance breaks down or whatever it is you need to fill out your tax forms. (I had that pleasure ahead of me, a first I wasn't especially looking forward to.)

The second carton hadn't been tied, or if it had, there was no sign of the cord on it or on the closet floor. I pushed both cartons back, took a look through the clothes on the rack and the things on the shelf, and left the room.

The study, as Mitchell had told me when we came in together on Monday morning, had once been his bedroom, so there was a closet there, too. A few clothes hung in it, but mostly it was used to store old papers. Each of these cartons had been untied. I looked in the nearest one and saw that it contained records for Nathan's business, which had been called Sleep House and had an address on Broadway. I wrote down the address, pushed the carton back in, and looked through the others. It was all very dull.

There were several unmatched bookcases in the study, one with glass doors that locked. The key was in the lock and I turned it, opened the doors, and looked at the books. A man who leaves a key in a glass-fronted bookcase is not hiding anything, but I looked anyway. Most of the books were in English, but some were in French, German, and what looked like a Slavic language that I did not recognize.

The other bookcases had books that were probably less costly. Volumes were crowded on the shelves, many stacked horizontally over the ones standing vertically. Even the tops of the bookcases had been called into service. There Nathan's paperbacks lay, piled one on top of the other in rows. They indicated an interest in philosophy, archaeology, logic, and politics. Like the educated man he had been, Nathan had never stopped learning.

I had been in this room only on the day we had discovered Nathan's body. Usually Nathan and I had sat in the kitchen over lunch or in the living room with tea. Had I been in this room previously, I surely would have asked him a lot of questions I did not think of asking without seeing his choice of books.

The last thing in the room was the desk. I sat at it and pulled open the top center drawer. There seemed nothing of interest there, no keys, no notes. I went through the three left-hand drawers, starting at the top. In the bottom drawer I found an envelope of snapshots. I wondered why they had been kept separate from the ones in the carton in the closet, but I didn't want to spend too much time looking. I was getting a little nervous about being there. So I put the envelope in my handbag and started on the right-hand drawers.

The top drawer gave me a start. When I had opened it last Saturday, the leather address book had been the first thing I saw. Today it was noticeably absent. I ran my rubber-gloved hand around the drawer, pulling bits of paper forward, but there was no book. What I did find was the triangular scrap of envelope with Nina Passman's address and telephone number on it. Someone had removed the book, and the little scrap of paper had fallen out.

I was about to pull out the second drawer when I heard voices. They were low and indistinct, but definitely two different ones. That was all I needed, to be found here by the police. If they arrested me, Arnold would kill me, but he would defend me. And Jack—I really wasn't sure what he would do, and I was perfectly content not to find out. I leaped out of the chair and ran for the kitchen, dropped the rubber gloves in the bucket, and walked into the hallway. I was still wearing my coat, so it would look as though I had just walked in—I hoped.

"Hey, Dick, lookee here," a man's voice said, and it came to me that if these were cops, they would not push a door open and call politely to see who was inside. They might well come in with guns drawn and nerves taut, ready to fire at anything that set them off.

I ducked back into the kitchen to stay out of the line of fire—just in case.

The door opened very quietly, and the men moved down the hallway as though they wanted to surprise whoever might be inside. There was no talk now, just a slight scraping sound. I wasn't going to be surprised, but I wanted to make sure I didn't get myself shot either.

"Hello," I called. I waited to make sure my voice had registered before venturing out of the kitchen to face two plainclothes cops with guns drawn. "Hi," I said.

"Bennett," Franciotti said without concealing his annoyance.

"That's me."

He holstered his gun. "What the hell are you doing in a crime scene? You got the key to this place?"

"No. The door was ajar when I got here, and I thought you might be inside. Someone broke in." I walked to the living room, and they followed me.

"Shit," the other one said.

"Musta come over the roof from the next building," Franciotti said, and I realized he was right. Nathan's fire escape was on the street, where someone climbing would be visible night or day.

The second cop had left us and was looking through the rooms. Now he returned. "Maybe he wanted a warm place to stay, Dick. Don't look like he did much."

''Would you know if anything's missing?'' Franciotti asked.

''I'm not sure. It looks pretty much the same as it did on Saturday.''

I could see he wasn't altogether happy with my presence there. ''OK. Can I ask you to leave now and not come back until we've finished our investigation?''

''I'm on my way.'' I gave what I hoped was a winning smile and left the apartment.

This time I felt safe going downstairs. Two of New York's finest were on the premises.

10

The thing I didn't know was whether the police had taken the address book or the intruder had. If the intruder had it, there was a good chance that his name and address were listed in it. That would certainly explain why the apartment had not been tossed. If someone who knew Nathan had killed him, the killer wouldn't expect the address book to be hidden in a carton of photographs or sewn into a sofa cushion.

I couldn't ask Franciotti without letting him know I had been snooping. But Jack might be able to find out what the police had taken from the apartment last Saturday. I thought of going down to Gallagher's and calling from there, but Gallagher worried about the price of everything, and a call to Brooklyn was more message units than he would want to squander. Nor could I offer to pay for the call without hurting his feelings.

I walked over to Broadway and called from the phone booth in the coffee shop. Jack wasn't there, and no one knew when he'd be back. I didn't bother leaving a message.

I pulled out my list of mourners and called the next one down after Hillel Greenspan, a couple named Zilman. A woman answered. I told her I was looking into the death of Nathan Herskovitz and could I come over and talk to her.

"It's my husband you want," she said, "and he's out for his walk."

"May I come over and wait?"

"No. I don't let anyone in if my husband isn't here."

"I'll call later," I said, and hung up, wondering how dangerous I sounded over the phone. I pulled another quarter out of my purse and called the next number on my list.

The man who answered, H. K. Granite, according to the book, wanted nothing to do with me. When I said I wanted to ask him some questions and could I come over, he said, "Ask them now over the phone."

"I'm calling from a pay phone, Mr. Granite. I could be at your apartment in ten minutes."

"I don't know anything. Didn't I hear they arrested someone?"

"I think it's the wrong man."

"Look, Miss—"

"I won't take much of your time. Ten minutes, OK?"

He said, "Ahh," in disgust, and hung up.

I didn't know whether that was a yes or no, but I decided to give it a try. He lived in the Nineties, and I was in the Seventies, so I flagged a cab and rode up. I could have taken the subway, but sometimes you wait ten minutes for a train, and when you travel off rush hour, it can get a little spooky. I mean, I look at those able-bodied men and I wonder why they aren't at work somewhere.

The taxi dropped me in front of an apartment house between West End Avenue and Riverside Drive. There was a Granite listed at apartment 4E. I rang.

A voice came over the intercom, and I identified myself. He buzzed me in, and I took the elevator up to four.

The apartment could easily have doubled as an art gallery. Every possible space on the walls was covered with a painting, and sculptures stood on pedestals and tables everywhere.

I thanked him for letting me in, and he grudgingly pointed to a chair in the living room. What distinguished him from all the other people at the funeral was his comparative youth. I didn't think he was more than seventy, considerably younger than Nathan's other cronies.

He lit his pipe with the kind of care pipe smokers take and said, "I don't know the first thing about Nathan's death. I opened the *Times* on Monday, I saw the obituary, I went to the funeral. If you came up here just to hear that, you could have heard it over the phone."

"How long did you know Nathan?" I asked.

He shrugged. "Forty, forty-five years."

"You met him in New York?"

"In the late forties. We were all part of a group."

"What kind of group?"

"Old countrymen. We shared a language and a background. We had dinner together at this one's apartment, that one's apartment. We talked, we laughed, we made new lives."

"Who was in the group?"

He rattled off names, most of which I had on my list. After some he added, "He's gone now," or "She died years ago."

"Did you know Mrs. Herskovitz?"

"Of course I knew her. He came to dinner, she came to dinner."

"What was she like?"

"She was a nice woman."

"I've heard she was sick."

His lips pursed, his shoulders moved. "I never heard that."

"She committed suicide."

"Some people couldn't adjust."

He sounded very offhand, as if he couldn't care less. If you couldn't adjust, you committed suicide. Simple as that.

"Did you know Nathan had a wife and children in Europe who didn't survive the war?"

"Miss Bennett, I'm not a gossip, and I don't enjoy dredging up people's old sorrows. A lot of people lost families during the war. They did the best they could to repair their lives. If Nathan had a family that didn't make it, well, he did what he could."

"Was he a good husband, Mr. Granite?"

"A good husband," he repeated. "What do you know about Nathan Herskovitz? Yes, he was a good husband. He was nice to her, he took her places, they had a good time. Anything else?"

"Can you think of anyone who might have wanted to kill him?"

"Hah!" It was a loud, mirthless laugh. "Go see Zilman. He'll tell you."

Zilman was the name of the man I had tried this morning, whose wife would not allow me in. I told Granite what had happened.

"I'll call him myself. He'll open his arms to you. It's his favorite story." He got up and went into the kitchen, and I heard him making the call. There were a lot of pleasantries, inquiries about health, finally an introduction to my visit. When he got off the phone, Granite was all smiles. "Go," he said. "He's waiting."

I thanked him, gave him my phone number, and left, wondering whether he had done this just to get rid of me. Whether he had or not, the Zilman story was the most interesting one I had heard to date.

Mordechai Zilman was a short man with a white beard that covered the knot of his tie. It didn't cover the gold chain across his vest from which dangled what I took to be a Phi Beta Kappa key. When we were seated in his living room, he instructed his wife to bring fruit, which proved to be a godsend. It was two o'clock and I hadn't had lunch yet.

"So you want to hear about Herskovitz and the sacred text," Mr. Zilman said when the fruit bowl had been placed in front of me with napkins, a glass plate, and a little knife.

"I want to hear anything that might suggest a reason why he was killed."

"I can't tell you why he was killed. I can tell you why he was hated."

"Please," I said, reaching for an apple.

"In the last months before Nathan Herskovitz went the way of his brethren in Europe, he became a broker of human life. If you could pay for it, he could get you a document so perfect, it would make the real one look fake. He could make a German into a Frenchman, a young man into an older one, a clerk into a supervisor. So people got to freedom, and Nathan Herskovitz got rich.''

There was a pompous ring to what he said, and I found myself resenting his tone. I *liked* Nathan, and I sensed I wasn't hearing the most unbiased report of his prewar activities.

"What happened to all the money?'' I asked.

"I'm not his banker,'' Zilman snapped. "Maybe it's in Switzerland. Maybe he left it with someone he considered a friend only to find in 1945 that the Jews had no friends.''

"How was he able to accomplish these miracles, Mr. Zilman?''

"As I said, he was a broker. He did nothing himself. He found people to do the work. There are forgers who are very good at their trade. As it turns out, Herskovitz had defended one once and got him off with a light sentence. That was the man who made the documents.''

"That's probably where the money went then,'' I said.

Zilman stared at me for a good half minute. It was clear he wasn't used to being contradicted. He turned to his wife, who sat timidly on a dining chair just outside the living room. "Some water,'' he said, and she stood and disappeared into the kitchen.

I wondered how many decades this little woman had put up with this diminutive tyrant.

"Like other people whose main interest in life is money,'' Zilman continued as his wife brought a tray with two glasses and a blue glass bottle that produced fizzy water when she squeezed a gadget on top, "Herskovitz took better care of his possessions than he did of his family. He was a collector of rare editions. How many he had, I don't know, but surely a substantial number. To lose them would be a catastrophe for the literate world, and to leave them behind was to lose them. So he gave them away.''

"To whom?'' I asked. I sipped the seltzer and felt it go right up my nose and into my head. For a moment I thought I might sneeze and destroy Zilman's concentration.

"He gave a book to everyone he provided an escape for.''

"Were they to keep the books till Nathan showed up in America?"

"The books were gifts."

"Gifts," I repeated.

"Anyone who saved a book could keep it."

I felt a surge of affection for Nathan. "Do you have yours?" I asked.

I got another stare. I guess this little man must have gotten a lot of mileage out of staring during his lifetime—perhaps that's how he kept his wife in line—but I found him almost comical.

"Nathan Herskovitz did not assist me or my family in any way," he said, one hand moving to touch the gold key that hung from the chain.

He dropped his hand, set his shoulders, and continued. "But you see, he didn't mean it. It was only a ruse to get these poor fleeing people to carry out his collection."

"You mean he claimed the books after the war?"

Zilman gave me an acid smile. "I only know for certain about one book. That book was worth the entire collection. It was a fifteenth-century Jewish prayer book, an incunabulum, if you know the term. Even before the war it was worth thousands. Today it might bring half a million. A book like that should not be in the hands of a private individual; it should be in a library, where people can look at it and scholars can study it." He touched the Phi Beta Kappa key again so that I would know who the scholar in the room was. "The book had been given to Karl Henry Black—that was the Americanization of his name, of course."

Of course, I thought, wondering if he disliked me as much as I disliked him.

"About fifteen years ago Professor Black decided to retire. Academics are not the best-paid people in the world, and Black needed a nest egg to see him through his retirement. He decided to put the book up for sale through an auction house."

"Did you teach with Professor Black?" I asked, starting to get a feel for the source of his obviously secondhand story.

"I did." He paused to drink some seltzer. "I must tell you that before he did this, for many years Herskovitz had bothered him about the book, asking for it, threatening him, sometimes confronting him in the street as he went to and from work. Now, when the auction house announced the book would be up for sale, Herskovitz came in with the lawyers."

"To prevent the sale?"

"Presumably to prevent the sale, to challenge Black's right to own it, to disrupt Black's life as much as possible. I felt Black should have gone to court. He could have found enough witnesses to swear that Herskovitz gave the books away that no jury would have doubted him. But the judge halted the auction, and Black got nervous. He withdrew the book, and Herskovitz apparently then dropped the case."

"Then Professor Black still has it," I said.

"If only that were true." Zilman glanced at his wife, nodded to his empty glass, and waited till she refilled it.

My ire was really building. I couldn't imagine treating a servant the way he was treating her.

"On the day Professor Black took back the book from the auction house, he was found dead in the street."

"Murdered?" I said, my voice echoing my shock.

"Dead of a heart attack."

"And the book?"

"Gone."

"He may have died, and someone passing by picked up the package," I suggested.

"Then where is it?" Zilman countered. "A person who steals does so for money. Sooner or later the book finds its way into the hands of someone who knows what it is. Herskovitz took it, Herskovitz hid it. Maybe his children have it."

"I don't think so," I said. I couldn't imagine Nina doing her father a favor, and I wasn't sure Mitchell's relationship with Nathan had been strong enough that Nathan would have trusted him with something so valuable. Still, it was worth a couple of phone calls. "You didn't know Nathan Herskovitz, did you, Mr. Zilman?"

"Never."

"How did you happen to be at his funeral?"

"There was nothing in his life to celebrate, but his death brought a measure of justice. I went to celebrate justice."

I found this man so tiresome, I was ready to thank him for my apple and get up and leave, but I thought I ought to ask a few questions about the Black family. "Did you stay in touch with Professor Black's family after his death?" I asked.

"Not actively."

I had no idea what he meant, but I thought it would be purposeless to pursue it. "I wonder if someone in the family killed Nathan for the book." I just stated it, hoping he would pick up on it.

"I wouldn't blame them. Imagine how you would feel if your life savings suddenly disappeared, just at the time when you began to need it."

"If they killed him for the book, they didn't find it," I said. "The apartment wasn't searched."

"Surely you wouldn't seriously accuse a member of an academic family with so heinous a crime."

"I'm not accusing anyone yet. I'm looking for reasons why someone would kill a kind old man who never hurt anyone and who couldn't defend himself." I said it to anger him, and I succeeded. I could see him restraining himself.

"I told you the story not to place blame on the Black family but to give you an insight into a man's character. A person who becomes rich by brokering lives, who gives gifts and takes them back, is a man who cannot be trusted, a man who may well have antagonized other men to the point of uncontrollable anger."

I thanked him for his help and got him to part with the

address of Black's widow. Then I went to Mrs. Zilman and thanked her for her hospitality. She glowed with happiness. I hoped Zilman wouldn't take it out on her afterward.

11

I needed some food fast, and I got it on Broadway. The Zilmans lived on West End Avenue, the north-south street one block west of Broadway in the Eighties. When I finished my cheeseburger, I set out for the Greenspan address, which was about a dozen blocks south of where I was. I walked along Riverside Drive, admiring the view of the park and the river and New Jersey beyond. Fall had not yet made its colorful strike, but here and there a tree was losing its green.

I was so involved in my admiration of nature that I went right by the Greenspan building and had to turn back. A woman's voice answered the bell, and I was buzzed in.

Mr. Greenspan made a joke about my frequent visits, but I sensed he was glad to have the company. The woman who had opened the door brought us cups of hot chocolate when I had sat down, and Hillel Greenspan's face lit up in a way Mordechai Zilman's had never learned to.

"I have a lot of questions," I said after sipping my chocolate.

"I have a lot of answers," the old man responded.

"Did Nathan help you leave Europe before the war?"

"Nathan got for me and my wife identification papers so good, the Gestapo couldn't make better. You want to see them?"

"You still have them?"

"I have everything. What isn't back there is up here." He tapped his temple, stood nimbly, and left the living room, his cane thumping along. From the other room I could hear him humming. He returned quickly and handed me an envelope.

The photograph on the first document was of a young man with a resemblance to this old one, but not a clear match. The name was Herbert Genscher, and after the address, there were numbers that I took to be his height and weight in the metric system. There was also a long word that was probably his supposed profession. A raised seal gave it the look of authenticity that the military would so prize.

"Beautiful?" he said.

"It looks excellent." Of course, I had no idea what a real one would look like, but it didn't matter.

The other document in the envelope was for a woman with the same last name and a maiden name that I couldn't make out.

"Were they expensive?" I asked.

"Every week the price went up."

"Did Nathan make much on the transaction?"

"Nathan made nothing. He was a go-between, that's all."

"Between you and the forger?"

"With the forger and with the transport. He got a car, a truck, a hay wagon, whatever he could find, whoever he could bribe."

"Did he give you a book?"

"Who have you been talking to?"

"Mr. Zilman."

"You talked to Zilman?"

"A little while ago."

"What could Zilman tell you that I couldn't?"

"Mr. Greenspan, I'm just trying to find out whether someone who knew Nathan might have killed him."

"And you think Zilman did it?"

"I don't think Zilman did it. I don't know who did it. But Zilman told me an interesting story about a book."

"Zilman is a fool." He set his mouth and shook his head.

"Tell me about the books, Mr. Greenspan."

"What can I tell you? Books are sacred. Nathan had a collection of very valuable, very rare books. He gave them away to save them. Better they should survive in other people's hands than remain in his and die. He would say, 'Here, take it. A book like this belongs to the world, not to you or me.' "

"What about Professor Black's book?"

He shook his head again and wagged his finger at me. "Never think that a piece of the whole is the whole, young lady. If Nathan gave away a thousand books, it doesn't mean he gave away a thousand and one."

"I don't understand."

"Did you know Black?"

"No."

"Of course not. You're too young. Black was a second-rate scholar who got a good job when he came to New York because he had friends. In Europe he was nothing. Zilman is the kind of fool that Black could impress. Black was single when he left Europe. He was the perfect person to escort a woman and children. Nathan knew the time had come to leave. He knew he should go, too, but there was still work, people he had promised to help. He thought, a few days more and he would leave himself. A man on the run alone can take more chances. But for his family, time had run out.

"Black agreed to accompany Nathan's wife and babies, to look after them till Nathan joined them. But not out of charity. Black was not a charitable man. He wanted payment. They struck a bargain, and Nathan gave him the book."

"And he wasn't able to save them," I said.

"Wasn't *able*?" the old man nearly shouted. "He never came for them. He got on the truck himself and went to the border. He left them to die, a young woman and two beautiful children."

I could feel my skin prickling. I could imagine them waiting for the truck that never came, sitting, packed, with two sleeping children through a dark night, realizing finally at dawn that they had been had, betrayed, that there was no escape. If the story was true, it explained easily why Nathan had hounded Black for the rest of his life. But it didn't explain everything.

"How do you know this, Mr. Greenspan?" I asked.

"How do I know? You think I make up a story like this?

I know because my friend Nathan told me. I know because I knew all the people."

"Mr. Zilman said the book was put up for auction many years ago and withdrawn when Nathan went into court."

"Correct."

"Why didn't Nathan pursue the case? Didn't he want the book back?"

"Sure he wanted it back. It was his. But you got to prove these things when you go to court."

"And he couldn't?"

"There was someone who knew the whole story, but he was sick. The doctor said he couldn't testify. Nathan withdrew the case. The witness died."

It was all hearsay. I was inclined to believe Mr. Greenspan and disbelieve Zilman, but that was because I liked one and disliked the other; also because I wanted to believe good things about Nathan.

But hearsay or not, there was certainly a motive for Nathan to have hounded Black and for Black's heirs to want to retrieve the book.

"How much do you think the book is worth?" I asked.

"Who knows? Ten, maybe twenty thousand."

"Mr. Zilman said half a million."

"Zilman doesn't know what he's talking about. This is one book, not a collection. People don't pay that kind of money for books."

"Do you think Nathan had the book?"

"Somebody had it."

I smiled, and he smiled back.

"You think someone killed Nathan for the book?" he asked.

"I don't know. I was going to ask you the same thing."

"Anything is possible. Especially when you got people in New York who think a book is worth fifty times its value. So what else can I tell you, young lady?"

I said, nothing else today, thank you, and I took my leave. It was still too early for sunset.

* * *

I called Arnold Gold from home. I had changed into a stiff new pair of jeans and a plaid flannel shirt that I had bought from one of the mail-order catalogs Melanie Gross had thrown my way. Believe it or not, one of the big negatives in being a former nun from an order where a habit was required is that you have no old clothes. Every time I put on something to relax in, I felt as though I were modeling for the company. I look forward to the day when my fun clothes are soft and faded and losing buttons.

Arnold had just gotten home, and in the background I could hear his favorite music station, WQXR, playing what sounded like Mozart.

"So what do you got for me, Chrissie?" he asked.

"Plenty."

"Let's hear it."

"A lot of people may have loved Nathan, but there may have been some who hated him enough to kill."

"Don't give me conclusions. Give me facts."

I regaled him for the next fifteen minutes, admitting my once-over of the apartment this morning, including my discovery that the address book was missing.

"Cops probably took it."

"I'll ask Jack to check on it for me."

"So this guy Zilman thinks Herskovitz hounded the professor to death."

"That's the impression I got. It sounds like a real case of revenge."

"And we have a missing Jewish prayer book that could be worth ten or twenty thousand and could be worth half a mil."

"Depending on whom you ask. Maybe I'll go over to the auction house tomorrow and see if they have any record of an appraisal from fifteen years ago."

"Won't mean much," Arnold said. "Prices have escalated a lot since the seventies. But it's a place to start."

"Are you surprised to hear Nathan was a lawyer?" I asked.

"Can't say that I am. When we talked, I was impressed with the way he thought. He had a logical, disciplined mind.

He also had a lot of good ideas about how to handle Metropolitan. He would have made his mark in revenge law.''

I laughed. ''Is that the newest brand of law?''

''The oldest, Chrissie. The goddamned oldest kind of law anyone ever practiced.''

Jack called before I had a chance to call him.

''They told me a woman called, and I tracked down all the old girlfriends.''

''Before you thought of me.''

''How are you?''

''How are all the old girlfriends?''

''Changing diapers, if you want to know the truth. How's things?''

''Complicated.'' I explained about my little adventure this morning and the missing address book.

''First off, you can get your head shot off doing what you did this morning. Second, I'll check on the address book first thing tomorrow. So you think Herskovitz was killed over a book?''

''I think he may have been a tough guy to love, Jack. He may have angered a lot of people, not just his family.''

''Well then, where the hell have they been all these years? Why'd it take till now for someone to kill him?''

''I don't know.''

''It doesn't sound right.''

''I just have to take it where it goes.''

12

The case of the five-hundred-year-old prayer book that was withdrawn from auction had made the kind of mark that left people with sharp recollections. The man who had headed the book division of the auction house fifteen years earlier, Jonathan McCandless, had since advanced to a position high in the administration, and he accepted my unannounced visit on Friday morning with a frown and a meaningful glance at his watch. But when I mentioned Karl Henry Black and the prayer book, his face relaxed into a smile.

"That was one I'll remember for a long time without going to the files," he said. "Do you know what book that was?"

"I was told it was a Jewish prayer book."

McCandless leaned back in his swivel chair, smiled to himself, then returned to an upright position. "At the end of the fifteenth century, for about thirty years after the printing of the Gutenberg Bible, a small group of books were printed that have come to be known as the incunabula. One of those was a Haggadah. Do you know what a Haggadah is?"

I shook my head. "I'm sorry."

"It's the prayer book used at the Passover seder. One incunabulum was the Guadalaxara Haggadah—that's with an X," he added. "It consists of only six sheets, that's twelve pages front and back, and it's printed in Hebrew letters. The cover is leather mounted on wood with raised bands and rich blind tooling of geometric designs. It was printed circa 1483. In other words, Miss Bennett, we are not talking about a

94

book; we are talking about the rarest of books, the kind of thing that sets your teeth chattering when you're near it."

"I can see why," I said. "Did you ever doubt Professor Black's ownership of the Guadalaxara Haggadah?"

"Not till we were slapped with an injunction."

"What precautions do you ordinarily take to assure that something so valuable put up for auction really belongs to the person selling it?"

"When you're dealing with antiques, you have limited resources in that area. Of course, if an owner has purchased the object himself and has a receipt, that's the best proof. But many people come in with Aunt Jane's pearls or a piece of furniture that's been in the family for generations, and there's really no proof it belongs to them except their word. If they carry it in, it's probably theirs."

"But the Haggadah was a famous book. Did you do any checking on it?"

"Many people keep the ownership of priceless objects a secret to protect themselves from theft, so it often isn't known who owns them. Professor Black said he had acquired it in Europe before the war. He was able to document a continuous chain of ownership that satisfied us, dating from his entry into the United States. He had no bill of sale, but then he had fled the continent at a difficult time. We were confident the book was his."

"So he brought it in and then what?"

"My staff and I looked at it to determine its value. We thought it would fetch close to fifty thousand, as I recall."

"That's a lot of money. Was Professor Black satisfied with your appraisal?"

"To tell the truth, he wasn't. I think he expected a sum that would enable him to retire. But that's not unusual. People often have an inflated idea of what their possessions are worth. He argued with me, but it was pointless. My appraisal is only an opinion. If you follow auctions, you may have observed that many items are sold far above their estimated value. I prefer a conservative evaluation. It leaves fewer people disappointed."

"So in spite of what he considered to be a low appraisal, he chose to go on with the auction."

"That's right. He consigned the Guadalaxara to us, and we placed it in the next rare book auction, which was a couple of months later. Since this was a very special book, we displayed it quite prominently in the catalog that went out to the collectors on our mailing list. And I must say that since it was such a prized specimen, there was quite a bit of talk about it even before the catalog was mailed."

"Did you hear any rumors that worried you?" I asked.

"Nothing until the day after the catalogs went out, when I got a call from our legal department. When I spoke to Professor Black a little later, I got the impression he expected us to defend his position. We don't do that, of course." McCandless smiled. "If there was a question of ownership, that was his legal problem, not ours as long as we hadn't sold the book. We told him that until he could establish clear title, we were simply unable to handle the sale."

"And that finished it."

"More or less. Lawyers never do things quickly and cleanly. It took a little while. To be honest, I expected the case to be much more conclusive than it was. The man who challenged Professor Black's ownership never pursued the case further, which surprised me, I must say, and eventually we were cleared to return the book to Professor Black."

"I've heard there was a witness who was too ill to testify for Mr. Herskovitz."

"Yes," McCandless agreed, "I think I heard something to that effect myself. As you can probably imagine, the whole world of rare books was buzzing over the incident. Both sellers and buyers got very nervous, anticipating challenges to their ownership. But it all died down. These things are not as unusual as all that."

"Tell me about how you returned the Guadalaxara to the professor."

"Yes, the return of the book." McCandless pursed his lips before continuing. "I urged him to allow us to send it by our special messenger service, but he would have none of it. He was a strange, distrustful sort of man. He said he would pick it up himself, and we made an appointment. He came, checked the book, signed for it, and took it. That was the last I saw of him. I heard on the news that night that he had been found dead in the street near his home. There was absolutely no evidence of foul play, and, of course, the Guadalaxara was gone.''

"Had it been wrapped?"

"Oh, quite. There was a box made specially to fit it."

"And he came for it alone."

"As far as I could see."

"Mr. McCandless, during the time when the rare book people were buzzing about the Guadalaxara, before the court prevented you from auctioning it, did you have inquiries from interested buyers?''

"Oh my, yes. There was tremendous interest. It was a very rare specimen, you know. As a matter of fact, privately I revised my estimate of what it would fetch. I wouldn't be surprised if it had brought seventy thousand at auction.''

"What do you think it might be worth today?"

"Ah." McCandless smiled. "Substantially more. It might go as high as four hundred thousand."

The number shocked me. Zilman had had a far more accurate idea of its value than Mr. Greenspan. "I wonder if you could give me the names of the people who were most interested in the book fifteen years ago.''

"I most certainly could not. Both buyers and sellers are accorded complete privacy here, Miss Bennett. Those are the kinds of secrets that will die with me.''

He sounded as though he meant it, and telling him that I thought someone might have murdered Nathan Herskovitz over the book wasn't likely to make him change his mind. "Over the years," I said, "have you had any inquiries about the Guadalaxara?''

"I have had inquiries," he said with a little smile.

"Then interest hasn't dried up."

"I would say it hasn't. Do you have any idea of where the book is now?"

"I wish I did," I said. But I didn't have the faintest.

I went back to the West Side, where I had left my car, and went up to see whether the police had finished with the Herskovitz apartment. Sure enough, the crime scene tape was gone, and the door to the apartment next door had been sealed with plywood. So much for security. It wouldn't take much to break in, but I supposed that was all Metropolitan Properties was prepared to do. I made a mental note to call Mitchell this evening and tell him what had happened.

I went down and said hello to Gallagher. He said he had seen two handymen from Metropolitan the previous afternoon and he had watched them fixing up the broken wall to Nathan's apartment and sealing up the door next to it. We chatted briefly and then I left.

On my first try, I didn't get very far. As Ian locked his three locks behind me, I heard the drumming I had heard on Wednesday. It was coming from one of the empty apartments that I would have to pass to get to the stairway. I stopped dead. I was on the third floor, two flights up from the lobby. I could probably make it if I tried. And if I went back to Ian's and asked him to call the police, whoever was waiting for me would be long gone by the time they came, even if they were nearby.

I decided to chance it. I pressed my left arm tightly over my bag and held my flashlight in my right hand. If worst came to worst, I had a weapon. Then I lit out for the stairs.

I didn't make it. He darted out of an open door, looking like a dark shadow in the unlit hall, and grabbed me. I took a deep breath and screamed as loudly as I could, hoping Gallagher would hear me. Then I pulled and tugged against my assailant, who was behind me and who slapped a hand over and into my mouth, nearly choking me. A dirty, smelly hand in or near your mouth is one of the more disgusting things you can experience. I came down hard with my teeth, hoping I wouldn't throw up. I heard an "Ow!" and then he moved the hand down the front of my body and squeezed my breast.

God forgive me, I was ready to kill. I screamed again, "Ian! Ian!" and pushed backward fast, hoping to force his body away from me. Then I raised my foot and kicked backward as hard as I could.

I don't know whether I hit anything vital or not, but at that moment Gallagher opened his door, said, "Oh, dear God, I'll get the police," in that wonderful brogue of his, and went back inside.

My assailant pushed me down and fled down into the stairwell.

The police came very quickly. I was downstairs by then with Ian, and I opened the locked front door for them. They tried to be helpful, but I was in the embarrassing position of not being able to identify the man who had assaulted me, or even describe him very well. Nor could Ian.

"You gotta be careful here, ma'am," one of the policemen said. "This is a dangerous building to be walking around in alone."

I knew that. I explained what my business there was, and he shrugged. I sympathized with his frustration. All he could do was tell me; he couldn't offer protection, and he couldn't keep me from entering the building. They promised to drive by more often and alert the patrol car teams on the next tour, but Franciotti had promised that last week, and what good had it done?

Finally, after answering all the questions required for the complaint report, I walked over to Broadway to use a pay phone. I wished I had access to Nathan's apartment, just for a place to sit down, use a bathroom, and look over my notes, but of course, he had given me the wrong keys or badly made keys and I had to improvise.

I started trembling as I walked, probably a delayed reaction. My mouth felt dirty, and I could still feel the pressure of his fingers on my breast, as though each one had left an individual bruise.

To calm myself, I had a cup of coffee in our favorite coffee shop and pulled out my list of Nathan's mourners. The next name was Strauss down on Seventy-second Street, and I had written a question mark for the first name. When I finished my coffee, I called Jack first and got him at his desk.

"Glad you called," he said. "I talked to a guy at the precinct and asked about your missing address book. They don't have it."

"OK." I suddenly felt a lot better. "That means whoever broke into the apartment took it. And I'll bet it means his name's in that book."

"Assuming you're right, how're you going to reconstruct the entries in the book?"

"I can't, but it means someone who knew Nathan killed him."

"Possibly."

I hate caution when I think I'm on a roll. "And it's even possible it was someone who went to the funeral."

"Also possible."

"And I've got all their names and addresses, and I'm interviewing all of them." I tried not to sound as smug as I felt.

"Terrific," the love of my life said dryly. "Every time you knock on a door, it's opened by a potential killer. You'd better check in with me before tomorrow night in case I need to look around for a replacement for dinner."

"You're overreacting," I said, stifling a giggle. "I haven't spoken to anyone under seventy so far, and the seventy-year-old looked like a kid compared to the others. I don't think old men commit violent murders."

"I just wish you wouldn't play Sherlock Holmes. Can't you be happy teaching poetry? Jesus, sometimes I think that sounds like the greatest life in the world."

"It is, but I cared about Nathan Herskovitz. If Arnold Gold thinks Ramirez may not be the killer, someone's got to

look into it, and I seem to have gotten the job by default."
My quarter dropped, and I started fishing around my purse
for more change.

"OK, we've both gotta go. I'll see you at six tomorrow."

" 'Bye, Jack," I said as the operator came on, rather proud
of myself for keeping the attack a secret from him.

13

I pulled out the battered phone book, found B. Strauss on Seventy-second Street, and called the number. A woman answered. I introduced myself and got a sign of recognition.

"You're the girl from the funeral," she said.

"Yes, I was there."

"So you were a friend of Nathan?"

"I was, and I'd like to ask you some questions. We're not sure the police have arrested the right man."

She agreed to see me, and I walked down Broadway to Seventy-second and then east toward Central Park. There are some fine old buildings there, including the Dakota, where I gather an apartment can cost a million dollars. Mrs. Strauss lived in one of the less affluent-looking buildings, but one with character nevertheless. I rode a shaky elevator up to her floor, and I heard the click of locks as I walked down the hall toward her apartment.

She was a modestly plump woman with a fresh, good-looking face and still-dark hair streaked with gray and wound up in a bun. We introduced ourselves, and she led me into a large living room with a grand piano that occupied a whole corner of the room.

"Do you play?" I asked when we had sat.

"It's not so easy anymore," she said, stretching out the fingers of both hands, then making fists and stretching them out again. "When you get to my age, a lot of things hurt, a lot of things don't move the way they used to. I still play, but it's not like it was." But even as she said it, her face glowed with a happiness that made me feel she had replaced her piano playing with something that gave her equal pleasure.

"I'd like to talk to you about the way some things were." I went through my little monologue about Nathan's murder and some of the things I was interested in. "Were you a friend of his?" I asked at the end.

"My husband knew him from the early nineteen thirties. My husband was a little younger than Nathan. If he were alive today, he would be eighty-one. I'm a little younger than that. I got to know Nathan in the late thirties, and of course, in a way, we owe him our lives."

"He helped you leave Europe."

"Not just us, a lot of people. But us, too."

"Did he give you a book?"

"Oh yes, a good one. Wait, I'll show you." She got up with agility, left the room, and returned with a book which she laid in my hands.

The leather cover was extremely worn, and I felt nervous holding it, as though it were someone's newborn baby. Gingerly I opened it about halfway. Most of the page was taken up with an illuminated letter. "It's very beautiful."

"Would you believe he wouldn't take it back?"

"I thought Nathan was a generous man," I said.

"There were times when he could have used the money. The first years in New York weren't the easiest."

"Mrs. Strauss, did you know Nathan's first wife in Europe?"

"So you know about Renata." She said it with resignation, as though she had already decided that that would not be a topic of our conversation. "I knew her, yes."

"Do you know the story of the person who was supposed to get her out and—"

"And didn't but accepted payment for it. I know. I wish my husband were here; he would tell you."

"You tell me," I said softly.

Her face took on a troubled look. Where Zilman had delighted in denouncing Nathan in his version of the story,

Mrs. Strauss was unhappy that Professor Black had done what she was convinced he had done. I got the feeling that it hurt her to recount the dishonorable act of another person, a person who should have been beyond reproach. "He was not a common laborer," she said at one point of Professor Black. "He was a member of the academic world. To us, that is sacred."

But her story was essentially the same as Hillel Greenspan's. Nathan had contracted with Black for the latter to escort the three Herskovitzes to safety, and Nathan had paid him with the Guadalaxara Haggadah.

"How do you know all this?" I asked when she had finished.

"Because Nathan Herskovitz was no fool. He had my husband as a witness to the agreement with Professor Black, and he gave the book to my husband, so that my husband would give it to Black when Renata was safe."

"Then your husband was the person who was too ill to testify in 1975 when Nathan took action against Black in court."

"So you know all that."

"I was at the auction house this morning, Mrs. Strauss. I talked to the man who was head of the rare book division fifteen years ago."

"Please," she said with a smile, "call me Bettina."

"What a lovely name. I'm Chris."

"Thank you. In this country I'm often called Betty, but I much prefer my given name. There was a famous woman in the Romantic period named Bettina."

"Bettina Brentano," I said.

Her face lit up. "So you know a little something about literature."

"A little something," I repeated. "Yes."

"That's good. It makes me feel closer to you. Yes, yes, it was my husband. You see, we were scheduled to leave with Professor Black and Renata Herskovitz and her children. We were picked up by a hay wagon, and we hid under the hay. We thought the farmer would go to the Herskovitzes after he picked us up, but instead, he went right to the border. We were being pulled by a horse and it was very slow, so it was hard to tell how far we'd gone. By the time we asked Black what was going on, it was too late to turn back. He made up some story about why he hadn't picked up Renata, but I think he didn't want the responsibility. At one point my husband attacked him physically. If you had known my husband, you would know how ridiculous that was. He was a beautiful person, but he hated violence; it repelled him. For him to grab that terrible man and shake him was a watershed in his life.''

"So the three of you made it to safety.''

"You put very simply what was really very long, very frightening, very complex, and very dangerous. Somewhere along the way some soldiers stopped the farmer and made him take a detour to get them somewhere they had to go. They actually got on the wagon on top of the hay, almost on top of where we were hiding. They were rowdy and drunk and disgusting, and we feared every moment that we would be found and shot—or worse. That's the way it was then with refugees. But yes, we made it to safety, and no, Renata and her children didn't. When I realized what had happened, I sat back and cried. I knew as surely as I see you now that I would never see her again.''

"It sounds to me as though Professor Black counted on that.''

"I'm sure he did.''

"But if Professor Black didn't fulfill his part of the bargain, how did he end up with the book?''

"As we climbed on the hay wagon, Black took the little bags we were carrying and pushed them in a corner. Sometime during the night, the book disappeared from my husband's bag.''

"You mean he stole it.''

"You could say that. We felt that he did.''

"If Nathan had pursued his lawsuit, he would have had a very strong case.''

"Without my husband, it was one man's word against the

other. My husband had had a heart attack earlier that year. He died in 1976, fourteen years ago.''

"Why didn't you testify?" I asked. "You knew the story."

"I didn't testify because I'm an honest person, and Nathan respected it. He couldn't ask me to perjure myself, even to recover that book. I wasn't there when the agreement was made. I actually never saw my husband put the Haggadah in his travel case, although he showed it to me when he came home. I never saw Black take it from the case. What would a lawyer have said? 'Your husband came home with a book that he later gave to Professor Black.' What could I say to that? Only that there are people I trust and believe and people I don't.''

"Bettina, something has been bothering me since I realized that the pictures in Nathan's living room were of his first family.'' Her eyes went up at that, but I continued. "He couldn't have kept personal possessions through the war. How could he have had all those pictures?''

Bettina Strauss smiled. "We took them for him. When my husband collected the forged papers, he offered to carry whatever Nathan wanted. It was understood that Nathan would follow us by a day or two, but he would travel light and alone. My husband said he scooped up the pictures in the living room, put them in a little sack, and said, 'Please take these.' Between us we distributed them in our bags, in my coat pockets, even in the lining. It was the least we could do. We owed him our lives.''

"And then you gave them back to him when he showed up in New York.''

"He asked for them.''

"Did Hannah know about Renata?" I asked.

You would have thought I had asked her something unanswerable. She looked uncomfortable, uneasy. "Of course she knew,'' she said finally. "When the war was over, Nathan was a man of forty. Hannah was younger, but she would have assumed he had had a family. Why do you ask?''

"Why did my question make you so uncomfortable?''

"I cannot explain to you how terrible those times were. People did things then that they would never have done in normal times. That my husband could become violent, that I could rob a dead body . . .'' She shivered, then became silent, and I regretted my question.

"Please don't tell me things you don't want to talk about," I said.

"I want you to understand. Nathan had a wife that he loved. She died. He met Hannah. He loved Hannah, don't think he didn't. She was a fine and beautiful girl, very beautiful. Of course he told her. Half the people who survived were left widowed. Nathan didn't talk about it, and I know he didn't tell his children. Was that right or wrong?'' she asked rhetorically. "Then was then and now is now. Today if you have a problem, you call a psychologist, and he spells out exactly what to do. Nowadays families tell their children everything. You don't tell them, you ruin their lives. Parents are afraid, so they do what the psychologist says. In the forties and fifties, it was different.''

"Did Nathan and Hannah have a happy marriage?''

"Very. I knew them.'' She said it with great certainty.

"I know she committed suicide,'' I said.

"How do you know all these things?''

"Nina told me. I don't think she ever forgave her father for the way he treated Hannah.''

"Ah.'' Bettina slapped her palms on her thighs. "Nina doesn't know anything. I told Nathan he should sit down with that girl, he should talk to her. She was so impressionable when Hannah died.''

"Bettina, Nathan's living room is filled with pictures of Renata and the first children. There isn't a single picture of Hannah, Mitchell, or Nina.''

"My God.'' She seemed genuinely surprised. "I haven't been in that place in I don't know how long. The building was in such chaos, you took your life in your hands if you went in.''

"I know,'' I said, still sore from my recent adventure. "But why do you think Nathan abandoned Hannah in his thoughts?''

She shook her head slowly. "He got old. He remembered the best times, the sweetest times. What else can I say?"

I felt I had worn her out by taking her back so far. She worked her fingers, opening and shutting her hands. "Would you play something for me?" I asked.

"You are a musician?"

"Not at all. I teach English poetry at a college in Westchester."

"Then I will play for you." She seated herself on the piano bench. "One movement of the Waldstein, a little slow, but you'll recognize it."

I sat back and listened. If she was in pain, it didn't show. Her face was shining. Her fingers moved nimbly. I listened to Beethoven's wonderful melodic line with rapture. In fleeing Europe she might have left behind a lifetime of worldly possessions, but this was one they could not make her part with. I felt very glad that I had asked her to play.

When she finished, she sat for a moment facing the keyboard.

"Thank you," I said.

She moved herself to the other side of the bench and faced me. "Thank you for asking. Playing is the best exercise."

I gave her my phone number and said I might be back. To my surprise, she kissed me as I left.

I found a nice, and thankfully different, place to eat lunch on Seventy-second Street. I was glad to see a menu not dominated by hamburgers. There were a number of older men and women there, and I wondered how many of them might have known Nathan, might have been part of his "circle."

Lunch was a marvelous salad with feta cheese and Greek olives, and I felt sated and happy when I finished. There were still a few more names on my list of mourners, but I wondered whether the stories would change very much, would add any new details to what I already knew. It must be a dull job for the police, who go from door to door in an apartment house asking the same questions over and over about one tenant out of a hundred or more, hearing almost nothing of value from most of the people they interview, or "canvass," as Jack calls it. Maybe it's because I know Jack or maybe it's just because I've given it some thought, but I feel sympathy for the members of the police department, especially because they take a lot of abuse and do a lot of necessary, unglamorous things that aren't appreciated or understood.

No one left on my list lived anywhere near Seventy-second Street. They were all farther uptown, some up near Columbia, which is roughly at 116th Street. If I drove, I would never find a place to park. It was Friday afternoon. Maybe I should give up for the weekend, drive back to Oakwood, drop in on my cousin Gene, who lives in a home for the retarded and whom I hadn't seen all week. It really sounded more appealing than getting on a bus or going down into the subway and asking someone else a whole bunch of questions that wouldn't get me anywhere.

I pulled my wallet out of my bag to pay for lunch, and I must have dislodged something near it. (My bag is the most disorganized part of my life.) What caught my eye was an envelope flap. I tugged at it, and up came a fat, open envelope. I said, "Oh" aloud, remembering that I had taken an envelope of snapshots out of a desk drawer yesterday morning in Nathan's apartment just as I heard the police arriving. After stowing it in my bag, I had promptly forgotten all about it. Fine investigator I'd make!

I pulled out the pictures. There didn't seem to be anyone I had met or previously seen a photo of. There were none of Hannah and none of Renata, none of any children at all. Several had been taken in what looked like a park or somewhere out in the country. There were trees, meadows, and benches. But the faces, men, women, and couples, were unfamiliar.

Until I looked at one near the bottom of the pack. The picture had been taken twenty, possibly thirty years ago, but the subject was easily recognizable, and seeing it, I gasped.

I took a ten out of my wallet, dropped a tip on the table, and went to pay the cashier. Now I knew what door Nathan's keys would open.

14

I walked back to 603, telling myself the intruder would surely have left the area when the police came, and started climbing stairs, listening hard as I went. The snapshot had been of a young Mrs. Paterno, certainly a lot younger than she was now. She was very thin, and her dark hair was everywhere. She was wearing a summer dress in a country setting, and if she wasn't laughing, at least she looked very happy.

I got up to the sixth floor and stopped a moment to listen and catch my breath. All was quiet. Then I went down the hall to her apartment and rang the bell. There was no answer and no sound inside. I tried again. I knocked. I called her name.

I found the two keys Nathan had given me before Yom Kippur, took a deep breath, and inserted the Segal in the upper lock. It went in and turned easily. I heard and felt the bolt snap open. My heart kind of pounded. I turned the key back and relocked the door.

Nathan had given me the keys to Mrs. Paterno's apartment. Nathan had known Mrs. Paterno *a long time ago*, long enough that an affair with her might have provoked his wife's suicide.

Had he given me the keys by mistake, because he always had them near at hand and they were the first ones he picked up? I must admit I had a hard time seeing Nathan—seeing anybody—involved in a relationship with Mrs. Paterno. I had been pleasant and courteous to her, and she had responded coldly, treating me like a lesser being, a messenger to do her

111

bidding, never inviting me beyond her threshold except on the morning I could not reach Nathan. And from Gallagher's infrequent comments, I could see he didn't think much of her either, even though he had the key to her apartment, which I assume she had given him.

What did I have besides a big disappointment? How could he have done it, abandoned the beautiful, young Hannah in favor of this cold, hard woman? I felt almost as slighted as if I had been Hannah myself.

I turned toward the stairs, pulled open the heavy fire door, and started down, my heart aching. It was absurd to think she had killed him, and yet . . .

I heard a sound and I froze. I had just reached the landing between six and five. There was no drumming, but someone was coming up the stairs. Not again, I thought, my fear returning. I moved quietly to the railing and looked down, but whoever it was was keeping toward the wall, and I couldn't see him. I didn't want to chance the roof—it's too easy to be thrown off—but I had Paterno's keys, so that was a possible sanctuary. I wasn't sure where he was, but maybe I could get down to five and out of the stairwell to temporary safety— unless whoever it was wanted to get into Nathan's apartment.

I didn't have time to ponder possibilities. I went down the remaining steps to five as quietly as I could. I was wearing low-heeled shoes, but I wished I had on my sneakers. At the door to five, I could hear the footsteps approach the next lower landing. I pulled the door open and heard it make its usual awful grating sound.

"Who's there?"

My heart stopped until I put together whose voice I was hearing. "Mrs. Paterno?" I called. "It's me, Chris Bennett."

"Oh, you. What are you doing here?"

"Looking for you."

I could see her now as she paused on the landing between four and five to catch her breath. "What is it?" she asked brusquely, and my feelings of dislike returned with a vengeance.

"Can we talk in your apartment? Or Nathan's if you still have the key."

"We'll go to mine."

We went slowly back up to six. As we went down the hall, I pulled the keys Nathan had given me out of my bag. In front of her door, I put the Segal in and turned it. "Shall I try the other one?" I said.

"I'm sure it'll work," she said coldly.

It did. I pushed the door open and stood back to let her go inside first.

She dropped her shopping bag in the kitchen, took her coat off, and hung it in the closet, but she didn't offer to take mine. I wondered what it would take for her to be minimally civil.

We went into her living room, and I took my coat off and tossed it on a chair, hoping she was watching. Her living room fascinated me as I saw it. The walls were covered with pen-and-ink drawings of the kind you see in newspaper ads for fashions at the department stores. I went over to look at them and saw that each was signed A.P., Amelia Paterno.

"You're an artist," I said.

"It's something I do," she said disparagingly. "It isn't what I used to do." She left it at that.

"Did you know Nathan gave me the keys to your apartment?"

"I made the assumption."

"I think he was trying to tell me that if something happened to him, you might be able to give me the answers."

"I don't know why you would think such a thing." She took a cigarette from a pack on an end table and lit it with a lighter that lay beside it. Then she sat down and crossed her long, slender legs.

I took the envelope of pictures from my bag and showed her the one of herself. "I found this in his apartment," I said.

I saw her tremble. "So you want to add scandal to murder, is that it?"

"I just want to know who killed him, and why."

"You think I did it?" Her eyes flashed.

"No, I don't. But you obviously knew him well. Maybe you have some idea who did."

"This is all nonsense," she said, exhaling smoke and pushing it away with her free hand. "A man was killed. Another man was arrested for his murder. I feel safer with that—what's his name?—Ramirez person off the streets. Why are you insinuating yourself where you have no business? Can't you leave the dead in peace?"

"Mrs. Paterno, Arnold Gold is convinced that Ramirez—"

"Arnold Gold," she interrupted, speaking the name with contempt. "What does he know? He'll defend that man and make a name for himself, and all the rich criminals in New York will flock to him. He's nothing to me."

"Nothing?" I said with a little of my own contempt. "He got you heat. He got you electricity. He got locks on the door downstairs."

She was quiet for a moment, and I saw the ash from her cigarette drop onto the carpet. I wondered how she had avoided killing herself all these years.

"You're right," she said finally. "He's been good to us."

"How did Nathan Herskovitz happen to have the keys to your apartment?" I asked quietly.

"You know all that. We each had the other's keys in case of trouble."

"That's not what Gallagher told me. Gallagher said—"

"Gallagher," she said with more contempt. "Mr. Gallagher is a very common person."

"And Mr. Herskovitz?"

Her mouth trembled again. "Mr. Herskovitz was a gentleman," she said.

"You had an affair with him."

"I am not going to discuss my personal life with you."

"Nathan's wife committed suicide about thirty years ago," I said. I looked down at the snapshot of a much younger Mrs. Paterno.

"And you accuse me of that, too? I drove his wife to

suicide and then thirty years later I killed him? I won't dignify those insinuations with an answer.''

Her reticence made me wary. She *could* have killed Nathan. She could have followed him into his apartment last Friday, gotten into an argument with him, grabbed something heavy, and taken it with her after she hit him with it and locked the door behind her. Even if she had been covered with his blood, she had only to walk up one flight of stairs, take off her clothes, and shower in her own apartment. The object that had killed Nathan might have been picked up by the garbagemen days ago. As for witnesses, this was probably one of the safest buildings in New York to commit a crime in. The nearest person to Nathan's apartment, Mrs. Paterno excepted, was Gallagher on three. *And Gallagher had told me that Nathan left the bench on Broadway first.* There was no one else in the whole building that Friday afternoon.

I tried another tack, anxious that she not perceive my growing sense that she might be a viable suspect. ''Talk to me, Mrs. Paterno,'' I said in as warm a tone as I could muster. ''I'm not here to hurt you.''

''I cannot talk to people of your generation.''

So that was it. I was too young to understand. I was one of those baby boomers, a yuppie who cared only for money and the expensive cars and clothes and vacations it could buy. I almost smiled. In June I had bought the first lipstick of my life, and I had to remind myself constantly to put it on when I went into the city.

''I was a nun for most of the last fifteen years,'' I said. ''I left the convent last spring. I've been working with Mr. Gold because I care what happens to you.'' I picked my bag up off the floor and took out my driver's license. The photo on it was my face, all smiles, surrounded by the brown-and-white veil of the Franciscan order. I handed it to her, and she looked at it, then at me. She returned it, and her face nearly collapsed. I held my breath, hoping I had broken through.

''I met him after his wife died,'' she said.

Well, OK, that's what I'd say in her position.

"At the mailbox downstairs. I was a dress designer in those days. I designed for young girls, juniors mostly. Amelia P. for Kleghorn. The Kleghorn family had been in the clothing business for years. They were old and respected."

I sensed that was important to her, that she work for an old and respected firm, not a bunch of upstarts or, heaven forbid, yuppies.

"What an interesting profession," I said, choosing my words carefully.

"It was interesting. It was challenging. I was able to raise my daughter comfortably on what I earned."

I had never asked her about the elusive Mr. Paterno, but obviously he hadn't been around very long.

"I remember when Mrs. Herskovitz died. Everyone in the building knew what had happened. She was one of many people I knew by sight." She stubbed out her cigarette, reached for the pack, but didn't light another. "I don't think we ever said anything to each other." Now she paused and lit a new cigarette, took a few puffs, and set it in an ashtray.

"I had come home early that day, the day we met," she continued. "Mr. Herskovitz was standing at the mailboxes, just standing, looking down. He wore a hat and an overcoat. It was as if he didn't know where he was or what was happening. I felt afraid. I thought he was ill. I said something to him: 'Are you all right?' Then I recognized him. He was the man whose wife had died. I said, 'You're Mr. Herskovitz, aren't you?' He nodded his head. He was a good-looking man in those days. I am not an impetuous person, but I put my hand on his arm and I said, 'Come up to my apartment. I'll make you some coffee.' He shook his head, but he didn't look as though he meant it. He didn't look as though he had any purpose at all. I said something else to him, 'Come for a little while,' or something like that, and he came. I unlocked the door downstairs, we took the elevator, we went up to my apartment.

"I made coffee and we sat in the living room—" she looked around "—right here, and we talked. He said how nice it was that I had invited him. He had come home early to be home when his daughter got home from school. Since his wife died, he had had problems with the little girl. He was worried about her. I think she had found her mother dead.''

"She did," I said, remembering Nina's story.

"Such a terrible thing." She puffed thoughtfully on her cigarette. "We talked. Finally he looked at his watch and said he had to go. He put his coat and hat back on, as though he had just come in from outside. I felt so sorry for him, a man in his fifties, a wife who had committed suicide, all the responsibilities of the home now on his shoulders. I said if he ever wanted to talk to somebody, he should give me a call, come up, bring his daughter. After all, we both had daughters about the same age. I had no thought beyond a little friendly conversation, a cup of coffee.''

She stopped, and I thought of the circle Nathan had been part of, all those people from Seventy-second Street up to Columbia who surely opened their hearts and their hospitality to him when he needed it. He didn't lack for company. What he needed was a woman in his life, and there were no available women in the circle.

"What happened?" I asked quietly.

She closed her eyes and shook her head very slightly. "It happened differently," she said with her eyes closed. "He never came with his daughter, he never came when my daughter was home. We would arrange to meet in the afternoon, here." She closed her eyes again briefly. "We became lovers.''

"I see.''

"Do you?" She looked at me with her very dark eyes.

"Is that when he gave you the key to his apartment?"

"He gave me a key so that someone in the building would have it in case of trouble. I don't think he ever told his children I had it.''

"How long did it last, Mrs. Paterno?"

"We have had a relationship of sorts since that time.''

"I think he must have been a wonderful man to be close to," I said.

"He was. I only wish . . ."

I looked at her, willing her to go on.

"My daughter came home one day and found us—together," she said in a voice so low, I could barely hear her. "It was one of those days when the school closed early. I had forgotten. Perhaps I had stopped thinking about things like that." As she spoke, she started idly to pull pins from her hair, hairpins, I supposed; I couldn't really see them, but I could hear them as they dropped on a glass plate beside her. "She never forgave me."

I heard the tick, tick, tick as the pins fell. What an odd and interesting coincidence that was. Both Nathan and Mrs. Paterno had managed to destroy their relationships with their daughters irretrievably, and I wondered if the same reason wasn't at the bottom of both situations. If Paterno was lying and she and Nathan had begun an affair when Hannah was still alive, that might well have been who Nathan thought about as he sat in his chair during those evenings when Nina felt he had neglected her mother.

Or—and here I began to have a chilly feeling along my back—perhaps Paterno had been the second affair in Nathan's life, and the first had been during his marriage. A little while ago I had reflected that there were no available women in the circle. Perhaps he had had an affair with an unavailable woman. That kind of secret would be hard to keep. Hannah would have been sure to find out. . . .

As I watched, Mrs. Paterno pulled off the last of the turban and shook out her hair. A surprisingly large mass of black hair streaked with gray fell to her shoulders. I smiled.

She smiled back. "You like my hair?"

"It's magnificent. I don't know why you keep it wrapped up."

"It's a style," she said offhandedly, as though that was what we did this year; next year we'll think of something else.

"Did you visit Nathan in his apartment?" I asked.

"Sometimes."

"You knew the apartment."

"I knew it, yes."

"The police don't know what was used to kill him. Do you think if we went downstairs and looked around, you might be able to figure out what's missing?"

"Perhaps."

"You still have the key?"

She gave me a hard look. "I have it."

"Would you mind coming down there with me now?"

In answer, she stood, gathered her hair in one hand, and left the room. When she returned, her hair was tied girlishly with a purple ribbon. She had her handbag with her. I followed her out to the hall, where we stopped while she locked her locks.

In Nathan's apartment she braced herself before entering the living room. Once she was through the archway, tears formed in her eyes. She took an embroidered cloth handkerchief out of her bag and patted her eyes with it.

"It was something heavy," I said when she had put the handkerchief away. "It actually dented his skull."

"Please," she said angrily.

But I had said it for a reason. I wanted to see if she could be tripped up, if her sorrow was an act to persuade me of her innocence.

She looked around the room. The photographs were all in place. On one wall there was a mantel over a closed-up fireplace that had surely worked when the building was erected in the twenties but that, along with all the others, had been boarded up when it became too expensive to maintain them. There were several fairly lightweight objects spread out on the mantel, which I assumed the police had already examined for blood and whatever else might remain on them if they had been used as a weapon.

She shook her head as she looked, then went out to the kitchen. "It's very hard," she said, looking around. "He could have had a heavy frying pan, a trivet. There are many things in a kitchen that could be used for—violence. I don't know what he had here." She walked out into the hall and turned toward the bedroom. I followed her.

"It looks"—she shook her head—"the same."

We went to the study. "I don't know," she said, clearly tired of the whole thing. "There could be a hundred things missing and I wouldn't know."

"Thank you anyway," I said, disappointed.

"There was no need to kill him," she said, her voice hollow. "He was sick. He probably had less than a year to live."

So he knew and he had told her. Arnold Gold had told me that the autopsy had shown a tumor. Otherwise I would not have known.

"Mrs. Paterno, can you think of any reason that Nathan would have wanted to confess his sins last week?" I was aware that I was using a Catholic locution, but in this case, I thought it was appropriate.

Her eyes flared. "After all I've told you, you still think that my relationship with him was—"

"No, I don't," I interrupted her. "I don't think it was sinful, and I don't think Nathan thought it was sinful. I'm looking for something else. He wanted to go to temple on Yom Kippur, and his son told me he had never gone since the war."

"He was sorry for what happened between him and his daughter," she said. "Very sorry. I'm sure he loved her." Her voice broke as she said it, and I was sure she was thinking of her own daughter.

"Did he ever give you a book to look after for him?" I asked.

"What kind of book?"

"A very old one, hundreds of years old. It was very valuable."

"He never gave me anything."

I looked at my watch. It had been a long day, and I wanted to get on the road before the northbound traffic built up.

We walked to the door, and she locked it carefully. As we went to the stairs, I said, "If I can find you a place to live, will you leave this building?"

"I have no reason to stay anymore," she said. "I would leave tomorrow."

"You have my phone number, don't you?" I had given it to all three of them when I met them a couple of months ago. Gallagher kept it taped to his refrigerator.

She pulled a little book out of her bag. "Give it to me again."

I tried not to show my irritation as I dictated it. She had obviously tossed it out the first time, sure she would have no use for it.

We said good-bye on the stairwell and went in opposite directions. My descent was uneventful, and I took a good breath of air as I got out into the street, happy to be safely out of that place. Then I found my car, drove up to Seventy-ninth Street, over to the West Side Highway, and north.

15

The beat-up tan wreck didn't turn up anywhere as I drove. I kept enough of my mind on the road to look for it and insure my safe arrival home, but I was deep in thought all the way. Nathan Herskovitz had had a lover, a woman many years younger than he, a woman who had probably once come across as being quite beautiful, quite exotic, quite desirable. In the most romantic of ways they had met for secret afternoon trysts and thirty years later had still cared enough for each other that they remained in that terrible building, still secretly together.

A poem by Leigh Hunt that I had run across recently came to mind:

> Jenny kissed me when we met,
> Jumping from the chair she sat in;
> Time, you thief, who love to get
> Sweets into your list, put that in:
> Say I'm weary, say I'm sad,
> Say that health and wealth have missed me,
> Say I'm growing old, but add,
> Jenny kissed me.

Was it that, then? Amelia Paterno as Nathan's Jenny. I was bothered by the idea, and I was very troubled by Amelia Paterno's story.

By changing one small but very important detail, the time they met, I had a motivation for Hannah Herskovitz's suicide. She could have discovered her husband's infidelity, felt she could not deal with it, and taken her life. And Nathan, who sat apart from his wife on all those evenings in the fifties, may have been thinking of his lover one flight up whom he could not be with without causing disruption in his family and hers. It fit, but it troubled me.

Actually, two things troubled me. The first was something that tells you more about me than about the situation I was working on. When someone looks me in the eye and says, "I didn't do it," I am strongly inclined to believe him. When a defendant takes the witness stand and speaks in his own defense, I am moved. There is something very powerful about hearing a person declare his innocence. When Mrs. Paterno told me her story, I was strongly inclined to believe it.

But then there was the other thing. Jack had told me several times that when you work on a murder—he says homicide—you look for means, motive, and opportunity. Mrs. Paterno had a better opportunity than anyone else I could think of—including Jesus Ramirez—to kill Nathan. She had the key to his apartment. She could have been waiting inside when he came home from his bench in the sun. As for means, she could have picked up the weapon, whatever it was, used it, and disposed of it. Why hadn't she noticed something missing? She must have visited that apartment hundreds of times over the years. I racked my brain to think of some heavy object, a piece of crystal, a lamp that was no longer there, that could have dealt the death blow. But where was the motive? She already knew Nathan would not live out the next year. And if she loved him, *if she stayed in that awful building to be near him*, why would she kill him?

"Think, Kix," I said aloud, but nothing came together.

When I walked into my house, ready for half an hour with feet up and a look at today's paper, I opened the door to incipient chaos. The phone was ringing, and I dashed to the kitchen to answer it.

"Is this Miss Bennett?" a man asked in a less-than-friendly tone.

"Yes, it is."

"This is H. K. Granite." I had to think a minute. Granite was the "youngster" I had interviewed, the man I judged to be no more than seventy, the one who lived in the apartment crowded with art. "Are you behind these calls I'm getting?" He sounded downright accusatory.

"What phone calls?" I asked, pulling off my shoes and stretching my toes.

"You don't know anything about them?" He was still angry and sounded incredulous.

"I don't know what phone calls you're talking about, and no, I had nothing to do with them, whatever they are."

"I see."

I didn't. "You want to tell me about it, Mr. Granite?"

"I came in this afternoon and there was a message on my machine. A man said, 'I want the book.' That was it. About an hour later, he called back. He said he wanted the book and if I didn't have it, who did?"

"And you think he was talking about the book Zilman told me about yesterday."

"How do I know what book he's talking about? All I know is you ask who would want to kill Herskovitz, I send you to Zilman to tell you about the Haggadah, and suddenly I'm getting anonymous calls about a book that sound threatening."

"Did Nathan give you one of his books to take to the States?"

"He gave one to my parents."

"Your parents," I repeated.

"I was fairly young when we emigrated. By the time the circle was established in the late forties, I was old enough to participate, which I did when it met at our apartment."

"What happened to your parents' book?"

"I have it."

"Maybe that's the book he wants."

"I don't know what he wants. I just don't want to be bothered. You're sure you didn't give my number to anyone?"

"I'm sure. Did the man say he'd call back?"

"It wasn't clear."

"Would you tell me if he does?"

"I'll tell you and I'll tell the police."

"Fine. As long as you keep me posted."

He hung up.

I hung up, too, irritated by his tone and manner, and walked in stockinged feet to the living room. I pulled off my ruined panty hose and sat down with the paper, but I was not to have my rest. The phone rang again and I went to answer it.

"Is this Christine Bennett?" a rather odd, tight voice, a little high-pitched but surely male, asked.

"It is. Is this Mr. Greenspan?"

"You know me already?" he asked in answer to my question.

"Sure I do. How are you today? I haven't seen you in a while."

"The dinner is cooking and I'm getting ready for the sunset."

"That sounds nice." I waited. Surely he hadn't called to invite me to dinner or a sunset.

"You remember we talked about a man named Zilman?"

"I remember."

"And about books?"

"I remember that, too."

"Today I got a phone call."

A little heartbeat skipping. "Yes?"

"About a book."

"Tell me about it, Mr. Greenspan."

"What's to tell? A man calls, he says, 'I want the book,' I ask him what book, he says, 'You know what book. Where is it?' I say, 'First you tell me what book, then I tell you where you can find it.' "

"And what did he say?" I prompted.

"He hung up."

"No."

"Sure. He wants it, I don't have it, he hangs up. That shouldn't happen?"

"Mr. Greenspan, if he calls back, would you tell him you've thought about it and you'd like to meet him and talk to him?"

"I should talk to a stranger about a book I don't have?"

"It's possible Nathan was murdered for that book he had."

"You mean the book he didn't have."

"Yes, that's the one I mean. If you make an appointment to meet this man, I'll come along."

"Should I make an appointment with this murderer in my own apartment or you think it's better I should meet him in a street somewhere when it's dark?"

I really loved this old man. There was nothing wrong with his mind. At this moment, I had the feeling it was functioning a little better than mine. "I don't want you placing yourself in jeopardy," I said, trying not to laugh. "If you make an appointment for him to come to your apartment, I'll have the police there. How's that?"

"That could be OK if they have the time and they remember to come."

"They'll come. Make it anytime except Tuesday morning." I had to teach my class, murderer or no. "Is that all right with you?"

"With me it's all right. We'll have to see how the murderer likes it."

I made him promise he'd call if he heard from the man again, and then I got off the phone. Was someone else going through the list of mourners as I was? It had to be someone who had been at the funeral. Zilman? No, Zilman knew them all, if not personally, then at least by name through his contact with Black and Granite. And I had a strong feeling that just about everyone at the funeral knew everyone else.

But Granite and Greenspan were almost certainly in Nathan's address book. Granite and Greenspan. Maybe someone was going through the book page by page, looking for *the* book or looking for any of the books in Nathan's original collection. Maybe Nathan had been murdered over the book after all.

I pulled out my list of mourners. Gallagher and Paterno

were there, but I was pretty certain Nathan wouldn't have put Paterno's name and phone number in his book. And anyone who knew the slightest thing about names would recognize those two as not being part of the wider circle whom Nathan had helped to freedom.

I didn't want to call the remaining names on my mourners list, which were all further along in the alphabet than G, until I had met them. But there was Strauss. There was a chance, if I got to Bettina quickly, that she might not yet have gotten a call. I dialed her number.

She sounded glad to hear from me. I told her quickly what I was after.

"No one has called," she said. "Of course, I'm not home the whole day. Today I went to the Museum of Modern Art."

"Bettina, if someone calls, tell him you have to ask your daughter, and ask for his phone number."

"And you're my daughter?"

"If you don't mind."

"I would love it," she said.

"If he won't give you his number, and he probably won't, tell him to call you back the next day. Then we can arrange to meet him and I'll inform the police."

"You think this man killed Nathan?"

"I don't know. The man I spoke to at the auction house this morning said people are still calling about the Guadalaxara Haggadah. Maybe there's a crazy collector out there who's tired of waiting, and willing to kill for his collection."

"All right," Bettina said. "I'll do what I can. I suppose anyone who calls has my address, too."

"Nathan's address book was stolen from his apartment this week. I think this person may be calling everyone listed."

"So we're all in trouble, right?"

"Let's hope not. Bettina, I have one more thing to ask you. It's a question that may trouble you, but I want you to be honest."

"You make it sound very mysterious."

"It isn't mysterious. It's just a little uncomfortable. I want to know if you know or heard or thought or felt that Nathan was having a relationship with someone besides his wife in the fifties.''

"I can answer that very easily. I didn't know, I never heard, and it never occurred to me. I think he was a faithful husband.''

"I'm just looking for a reason why Hannah committed suicide.''

"There are lots of reasons for suicide besides an unfaithful husband.''

"I know that, but I've heard a bunch of conflicting stories. Nina says Nathan ignored her mother to the point of abuse. Mr. Greenspan says—''

"You saw Hillel? How is he?''

"He's fine. He says Hannah was a sick woman. Someone else says Nathan treated her well and there was nothing wrong with her.''

"Who said that?''

"H. K. Granite.''

"Ah, Henry.''

"I wonder if he was even old enough to have a valid opinion,'' I said, remembering what he had just told me about being quite young before the war and joining the circle when it met at his parents' apartment.

"He was old enough,'' Bettina said.

"OK. That's it for tonight.''

We concluded our conversation, and I started puttering around to make something to eat. I'm still not very adept in the kitchen, having left Aunt Meg's home for St. Stephen's when I was fifteen, an age when I might have just become interested in cooking. Also, I live pretty modestly, so things that I read about, like balsamic vinegar and sun-dried tomatoes, are beyond even my fantasies. My income comes from what remains of my dowry at St. Stephen's, some of which was used to buy my car and maintain it, from what Aunt Meg left me when she died last spring, and from the pittance I get teaching. I'm very happy with the way I live, and my expenses are pretty low. The house is paid for, and except for the clothes I had to buy to replace my habit, I really need very little. This is all by way of explaining why I eat more tuna fish than steak.

Anyway, I found some stew in a pot in the freezer, and I put it on the stove over a small flame, hoping it would thaw and heat before I died of malnutrition. Then I called Arnold.

When he answered, I heard his music in the background and knew he was in his study. I told him what I'd learned about Paterno.

"So our friend Nathan was a horny old bastard," he said when I'd finished.

People don't usually talk to nuns—at least not to teaching nuns who live in a convent—that way, and no one had talked to me that way since I'd left, so I was a little taken aback. I also didn't like to hear Nathan described so crudely. "Stop it, Arnold. It started thirty years ago when he was fifty-five. That's not exactly old, is it?" Arnold's about a dozen years older.

"Not from where I'm sitting. She said it right to you, that they had an affair?"

"She said, 'We became lovers.' Same thing, right?"

"Right on the button. How'd you do it, Chrissie? She's the tightest-lipped woman I've ever met."

I thought of my driver's license. "Just a trick of the trade," I said. "Arnold, do you suppose she could have killed Nathan?" I gave him a brief summary of my means-and-opportunity theory.

"But why? You just told me she knew he was dying. What's in it for her?"

"I don't know. I suppose I'm reaching, but when I discovered there was a relationship there, a whole part of his life connected to her that had been a secret for thirty years, I started wondering. Anyway, it's only one possibility. I went to the auction house this morning and inquired about the book." I told him everything, although I hadn't meant to. Planning to meet a possible murderer in an old woman's apartment—or an old man's—is not exactly everyday living.

He warned me, as I knew he would, but he seemed to feel

more certainly than I did that I was getting somewhere, that I knew more than the police (although anyone with brains would, he added gratuitously), and that if I kept at it, *we* might just find out who killed Nathan. In the meantime, he was trying to get Ramirez out on bail ("Do you have to?" I asked), and the rest of the world was hunky-dory.

As we hung up, I started to smell my stew, and I grabbed a spoon and stirred it around. The chunks of meat were still hard as ice beneath the surface, but the smell indicated promise.

While I was waiting, I called Nina Passman.

"Have you learned anything?" she asked after I'd identified myself.

"Quite a bit," I said, not wanting to tell her about the Herskovitz-Paterno alliance. "I have a few questions if you have a minute."

"I have just about ten."

"When you were in grade school, did you know a girl named Paterno?"

"Oh yes," she said immediately. "Julie or Julianne, something like that. Juliana," she said, remembering.

"Were you friends?"

"We knew each other. We lived in the same building, you know. Sometimes we would walk home from school together. But I wouldn't call us friends."

"You never visited her in her apartment?"

"Not that I remember. And then she left the school."

"When was that?"

"Around junior high. Her mother put her into a Catholic school, and I really didn't see her again. May I ask why this is important?"

"One of the remaining tenants in the building is a Mrs. Paterno, and she mentioned that she had a daughter. I was just curious about whether you knew her. There's something else that's much more important," I hurried on. "Do you know if your father's apartment was ever robbed?"

"Mitchell said something to me once. It was quite a while

ago, ten or fifteen years. I think a neighbor found someone trying to break in and called the police.''

"So they never got in.''

"I don't think so, but you ought to ask my brother.''

I told her I would, and I got back to my stew. I had known that Mitchell was a better source of information about her father than she was, but I wanted to ask her about the Paterno girl, and I didn't want that to be the whole subject of our conversation.

I put a fork in a chunk of stew and decided it wasn't ready yet, so I called Atlanta. A woman answered, and I told her who I was and asked for her husband.

"He hasn't come home from work yet," Mrs. Herskovitz said. "Would you like him to call you?''

"I'd appreciate it," I told her. I gave her my number again and finally sat down to dinner.

Mitchell called back about eight-thirty. I told him that the crime scene tape was gone and then let him know about the break-in. The police had not informed him.

"What on earth do they want?" he asked.

"It could have been anything. Buildings that are almost empty are very insecure, and break-ins aren't all that unusual. A friend of mine who's a policeman tells me they may just have been after the brass and copper plumbing for its junk value. I wanted to ask you whether anything like that had ever happened before.''

"You mean a robbery?''

"Yes.''

"There was one big one about fifteen years ago, I remember.''

"Fifteen years ago?''

"Around the time of the court case. Do you know about that?''

"Yes.''

"Well, we assumed someone in Professor Black's family or employ came looking for Pop's book. Frankly, I think our idea was a little farfetched. The Blacks had one child who lived in California, not exactly a second-story man. We heard through the grapevine that Mrs. Black had washed her hands of the whole thing.''

''Was Zilman the grapevine?'' I asked.

''You know Zilman?'' He sounded surprised.

''I met him yesterday. He gave me his side of the story.''

''No matter what happened, what good would it have done the Blacks to get the book back? My father could have gone back into court and prevented them again from selling it. All they wanted was the money.''

''Maybe there was a collector out there who just wanted to own it, just wanted it in his possession. There are people like that.''

He was silent for a moment. ''I hadn't thought of that. You think it's possible that someone's still after the book, that they killed my father for it?''

''I just don't know, but it's possible. Mitchell, how did your father explain the book to you?'' I was treading on sensitive territory. Nathan's first family had been Nathan's secret.

''He said he gave it to someone before the war, this Professor Black, to take to America for him. When the war was over, Black refused to give it back.''

''That's only partly true,'' I said. ''The book was to be payment for taking your father's first wife and children to safety. The story I heard is that Black took the book and left the family behind.''

''My God.'' It was a whisper.

''Do you think your father was capable of hounding that man Black for years until he finally died of a heart attack while he was carrying the book home?''

''There was a very dark side to my father,'' Mitchell said in a low voice. ''I think he could have done that. I think he could have done worse.''

''Do you know whether he ever had that book in his possession?''

''Not that I know of.''

''And he didn't give it to you to keep?''

''Never. I don't even know what it looks like.''

"OK. Tell me, Mitchell, can you think of anything heavy, anything that could have been used as a weapon, that was missing from the apartment when you saw it on Monday?"

"It's just so long since I really visited that place. The living room was arranged differently. He must have moved furniture around. And those pictures. It just isn't the place I remember."

I decided that was about all I could hope for tonight, and I finished the conversation. Then I did what I should have done days ago; I sat down with my notebook and read over my notes.

It was right there on day number one of my investigation. I had sat in the coffee shop with Ian Gallagher and begun my questioning with him. And he had told me in so many words that Nathan had complained of annoying phone calls.

I sat back and looked at what I had written. "It was a phone call now and then. They were bothering him. [Herskovitz] called them something in another language."

Phone calls, bothering him. Did somebody think he had a book or that he knew where it was? Maybe Bettina and I would find him.

16

I didn't sleep very well. Sometime around two in the morning the sound of the town alarm awakened me. Seconds later I heard sirens approach, and almost immediately my doorbell started ringing and someone pounded on the door.

The fire engines were turning in to Pine Brook Road as I got out of bed, calling, "I'm coming," threw on my robe, and went downstairs. My bedroom faces the backyard, so I had not seen anything unusual, but as I came down the stairs, I could see light through the living room windows. *Something was burning on my front lawn.* I opened the front door to find my next-door neighbor, Don McGuire, standing there, hair tousled, a raincoat over his pajamas.

"Come on out," he said. "There's a fire."

I got my raincoat and keys and went out with him. The flame was very bright, about halfway between the house and the street. I knew immediately it was no accident. Someone had set it.

"Midge got up to go to the baby and she saw it."

"Thank you both."

"You sure you're all right?"

"I'm fine."

"Damn kids. Looks like Halloween's a little early this year."

I didn't think it was Halloween.

The fire engines had arrived, and Oakwood's raincoat-clad volunteers had hooked up a hose to the hydrant across the street. Neighbors were coming out of their front doors, clustering there or walking toward my house. Don and I joined

Midge in front of theirs and watched as the firemen hosed down the fire. It didn't take long. After a few minutes there was nothing but a smoldering spot in the middle of the lawn and a smell of gasoline. I would have to reseed in the spring.

The fire chief came over and talked to me. He, too, was pretty sure it was a pre-Halloween prank.

"Will you find them?" I asked.

"Not unless we catch them in the act somewhere else. These kids are pretty slippery. I wouldn't count on it."

"Chief," I said, "it may not have been a prank." I started to tell him about my being followed the other day.

"This sounds like police business," he said before I'd gone on very long. "Come over here."

Two police cars were parked in front of the McGuires', lights rotating on their roofs. I gave a statement to both of the officers. (In Oakwood only one policeman rides a car. They don't expect the kind of danger New York cops regularly encounter.) They took me very seriously and promised they would drive by my house frequently until the Herskovitz murder was solved. I felt a lot more confident hearing their promise than I had hearing a similar one in Manhattan after my attack.

I thanked the McGuires again for their vigilance and went back to bed, to think more than to sleep. He had followed me after all, and he had sent a message. The only thing was, I didn't know what the message was. Keep away from 603? Leave the Herskovitz murder alone? Stay out of the book business?

I didn't know, but I was pretty sure I'd find out. Eventually.

I got my shopping done early on Saturday morning, stocking up for the coming week, which was starting to look pretty busy. Then I drove to Greenwillow, a group home for retarded adults where my cousin Gene lives. Whenever he sees me, he gives me the warmest smile of anyone I know and says, "Kix!" with great enthusiasm. Gene is responsible for my nickname, having come out with it at an early age when

my mother tried to get him to say Chris. I've always liked it.
I've met a lot of Chrises in my life, but not one other Kix. It
sets me apart.

I took Gene out for lunch, agreeing to McDonald's because it's his favorite. By the time we got back to Greenwillow, his enchantment with me had faded and he was ready
to join a group activity. I drove the ten miles back to Oakwood, looking forward to the new year when Greenwillow
would move into town, and spent some time cleaning up the
yard and chatting with neighbors who were outside doing the
same thing.

At three I lay down for a nap. My night had been badly
broken up, and I get up pretty early in the morning without
trying, the result of fifteen years of chapel at five-thirty, and
that leaves me near collapse fairly early in the evening. It
doesn't bother me on weekdays, but it's not too nice to conk
out on a date who's made a long trip just to see you.

I was showered, dressed, ready, and eager to see him fifteen minutes before six, but he was late. I had known him
about three and a half months at that point, and we'd been
going out for most of that time. I keep hearing about the
trouble women have finding datable, marriageable men, and
I, who wasn't looking for one, walked into a precinct house
in Brooklyn three weeks after being released from my vows
and found Jack. The relationship produced a few crises of
conscience for me. I had made certain promises to myself,
among them that I would not become involved with a man
until a decent period of time had elapsed after leaving St.
Stephen's, and I didn't think a month was very decent. Partly
I needed to know that I had left for the reasons I had stated
to my General Superior and later in a letter to the Pope. (St.
Stephen's is a pontifical community, and permission from
the Pope is necessary before you can be released from your
vows.) And partly I wanted the people at St. Stephen's to
know that I hadn't rushed into the arms of a man as soon as
I had left my habit behind.

But none of these things could keep me from feeling the
way I felt about Jack. I had gone out with Mark Brownstein

last Saturday partly to keep myself away from Jack for one weekend and partly because I had reservations about committing myself too soon and too completely to the first man I had ever dated in my life.

We were both thirty, but from something he had said, I had the impression that my birthday came earlier in the year than his, making me a tiny bit older. He had gotten a college degree by going to school nights for seven or eight years while on the job, and last month he had begun law school. I had the feeling it was tougher than he had expected, or at least different. I liked the idea of his becoming a lawyer. He would probably never do the kind of work Arnold Gold does, but they're pretty different kinds of men.

I was surprised that he was late. He tended to the early side, at least when he came to see me. Waiting generated a small amount of worry and increased my already powerful sexual tension, which I had promised myself again and again I would not give in to in this calendar year.

At six-fifteen I saw his car pull into the driveway, and I went to open the door. We kissed and kissed again when he came in.

"Sorry I'm late," he said. He stood in the center of the living room and looked distracted.

"What's wrong?"

"I got picked up for speeding on the Hutch."

I kept myself from laughing. "He didn't give you a ticket, did he?"

"I let him see my ID. I got away with a friendly warning."

"Thanks," I said.

"For what?"

"For speeding to get here."

He gave me the nice smile, took my hand, and we sat on the sofa. "What burned on your lawn?"

He sees everything, even in the dark. "The police think it's a Halloween prank."

He looked skeptical, but he dropped it. "What a week," he said.

He griped for about twenty minutes. Everything had gone

wrong, the car he and his partner drove, a lost report, a disagreement with the lieutenant. Worst of all, he had gotten stuck on a case on a night that he had law school, and he had come to class half an hour late, and the professor had attempted to ridicule him. Jack doesn't take kindly to that kind of treatment.

"I told him why I was late, and I didn't say it as if I was talking to my best friend. It probably cost me the course. He's not gonna forget me."

"He'll be fair. He's a lawyer."

Jack looked at me as if I'd denounced the flag. "He's a shit," he said between his teeth. He stood up. "Come on. Let's get out of here. I have to stop this."

We went to a restaurant in White Plains, which isn't far from Oakwood, and had a good dinner, but it wasn't a good night. It started out all right. He loosened up a bit, and I was glad he'd gotten the law school stuff off his mind. But it wasn't over.

After a taste of the main course, he said, "Why'd you have to go out with someone else last weekend?"

"I thought you understood."

"I don't understand."

"You're the first man in my life," I said, although we'd been through it all before. "I can't just see one man. It's a question of my own personal development."

"Shit. There are fourteen-year-olds who meet and go through life together—"

"I am not fourteen years old." It came out rather harsh.

"OK. I'll lay it on the table. You hurt my feelings."

"I'm sorry." I felt teary and awful. "What did you do last Saturday?"

"I did what I did," he said, not looking at me.

"I'm not going out with him again," I said. It was all very dumb. Mark was exactly the right kind of man to go out with. He was fun, and I wasn't going to fall in love with him. He was personal development with a capital PD and maybe, somewhere down the line, a friend. But I couldn't hurt Jack,

I couldn't jeopardize this relationship, which meant so much to me and which I had obviously already threatened.

"Why? Because it's not going anywhere?"

I almost got up and fled to the ladies' room, but somewhere in my head I knew that coming back would be even worse than staying. I took a hard swallow instead. "Because he's not you." I looked him straight in the eye.

"You'd better eat," he said. "And I'd better shut up."

It sounded like a good idea, and I returned to my dinner. It was the kind of food you only eat in a restaurant unless you're a very talented cook. Convent fare is not made by very talented cooks, only by hardworking ones trying to feed a lot of people within a tight budget.

He drew lines on the back of my hand with his index finger, and I smiled.

"You want to talk about your case?" he asked, all the fight gone from his voice.

"Just a little."

"You know, you may find out that this guy Herskovitz was Jack the Ripper, but it doesn't mean Ramirez didn't kill him."

"Arnold is really convinced—"

"Arnold Gold is a defense attorney. His client is always innocent, and the cops are always wrong."

"It's not that way this time."

"Chris, he'd defend Hitler if he had the chance."

"He wouldn't," I said, sounding stony.

"Then he'd find someone who would."

I thought he was probably right. "That's because he believes that everyone has the right to counsel."

"In this case it's because he wants to put a knife in the police department."

"Jack, you've got Arnold all—"

"Arnold Gold thinks every cop in New York is dumb and on the take. Well, he's wrong. I'm not dumb and I'm not on the take."

"I know."

"How?"

"Because I know you."

The waiter was standing over us.

"Yeah, I'll have coffee," Jack said. "You?"

"Please."

We drank our coffee uncomfortably and went out to the car. I felt the smartest thing was to keep quiet. If my Saturday night with Mark had prompted all this, anything I said would make it worse. If it was something else, I didn't want to pry. When it suited him, he would tell me. In the meantime, I sat quietly and coped with my feelings. I didn't know what we'd been fighting about, but nothing we'd talked about had been neutral.

We drove to Oakwood silently, but when he pulled into my driveway, my resolve left me.

"What is it, Jack? Something's eating you. I've never seen you like this." I said it quietly. I didn't want another unreasonable confrontation.

He turned the motor off but left the key in the ignition. "It's that fuckin' law school," he said so low, I could hardly hear him. "I'm sorry. I shouldn't do this to you. It's not your fault."

"What is it?"

"I don't know." He sat back. "It's harder than I thought it would be. It's more work. It's different. I'm not getting it the way I should."

"Give it time."

"Maybe." He fingered the keys. "In college, if I put my mind to something, I got it. I'm not afraid of work. This is just different. Maybe it's not for me. Maybe it's for people like Arnold Gold."

"It is for you."

"Why?"

"Because you set your heart on it."

"You still think I have a heart?"

I nodded. "Yes." It came out in a whisper.

He touched my hand. "I'm not coming in."

I gathered my purse and gloves and reached for the door handle.

"Chris." He pulled me toward him before I opened the

door, put his arms around me, and just held me. It was one of those stupid cars with the stick shift and stuff between the front seats. Getting close was almost impossible below the shoulders, but we did our best. I was so relieved that I was only one small part of what was bothering him that I felt absolutely happy. We kissed, and he brushed away what might have been tears on my face.

"We OK for next Saturday?" he asked.

"Yes."

He started to say something about picking me up when I remembered Mitchell. "Nathan's son and daughter-in-law are coming in next Friday night," I said. "I'll probably go down to the apartment to say hello. Why don't you meet me there? I'll stay over with Celia."

"OK."

"Will you call me when you get home?"

"Why?"

"Because you're a wreck tonight."

"I'm fine now."

"Please?"

He kissed me. "I'll call you."

He called so soon after he left that I was sure he must have gotten picked up for speeding again, but he assured me he hadn't. He said he was wide-awake now, ready to tackle his law school assignment for Monday.

17

Bettina Strauss called Sunday morning. She sounded tense and excited. "I got that phone call," she said.

"What did he say?"

"He asked if I had a book. I said, 'I have lots of books.' Then he gave me the names of a lot of people who had books like mine. I knew most of the names. They were members of the circle."

"What did you tell him?"

"Just what you said. 'I have to call my daughter.' He said he'd call back later."

"Do you feel up to it, Bettina?"

"You think this man killed Nathan?"

"I think it's possible. Or that he had him killed."

"Then we get him, right?"

"Right."

I outlined my plan, sounding a lot more confident about it than I felt. It called for making an appointment with the buyer for tomorrow afternoon. That would give me plenty of time to get hold of Franciotti. Bettina said the man had not sounded threatening at all as Mr. Granite had portrayed the caller, just that he was an interested buyer and knew she had something to sell.

Then I called the police station. Franciotti wasn't in, but he was expected tomorrow at ten. I left a message with my name, saying that it was urgent that I speak to him as early as possible Monday morning but that I would call him. I was afraid to wait in Oakwood for his call, cutting short the time

I would have to drive into Manhattan, find a place to park, get over to Bettina's, and get the two of us ready.

I spent most of Sunday preparing for my Tuesday morning class. There had been some discussion of the English Romantic poets, pro and con, and I had assigned some readings in their works. It was interesting to me that a couple of students seemed to agree that romantic equaled sentimentality which equaled garbage, while several other students looked blank when the era and the poets' names were mentioned. A little explanation was in order.

I am not enamored of Shelley, although he has turned a number of good phrases—"Hail to thee, blithe spirit!" and "Our sweetest songs are those that tell of saddest thought" come to mind—but anyone who can write, "I fall upon the thorns of life, I bleed," is not someone I can turn to for solace or understanding.

But Keats and Wordsworth really do something to me, and I was curious to know whether my young, ambitious women would agree, whether a healthy sample of poems would confirm or dispute their romantic/sentimental equation. Whenever I turn to Keats, I renew my amazement and admiration; I have already lived four years longer than he, and in much better health.

Bettina called back about four. "He's coming at two," she said. "He won't give me his name. When he rings the bell, he'll say he's the book man."

"OK."

"And if he wants the book, he'll pay in cash."

"I guess he'd have to if he wants to stay anonymous. How do you feel about it?"

"I'll tell you the truth, he doesn't sound like a murderer. He sounds like an older man who wants to buy a book."

"Maybe that's all he is," I said. "But where did he get your name from? And the other names he read to you? Somehow he's connected to whoever broke into Nathan's apartment Wednesday night. So let's be very careful."

"When will you come?"

"I'll try to get there when the parking restrictions end in the Seventies, about eleven. I'll be there a little after."

"Good. We'll have lunch together."

I agreed, although I was already losing my appetite. I couldn't think of this as quite the adventure that Bettina did, but then, I hadn't fled a hostile country in a hay wagon with a bunch of enemy soldiers sitting virtually on top of me. It must do something to one's outlook.

Someday I'll learn not to answer the phone when I don't want to talk to anyone else today, or just pull out the cord so I don't have to make any more decisions. But that's still in the future. Not long after Bettina called, the phone rang and I answered it. I still wish I hadn't.

"Chris, darlin'," a familiar voice said, "it's Ian Gallagher."

"Yes, Ian. What is it?" It was a toll call after all. He would only call if he needed something.

"Somethin's goin' on here," he said. "I thought Mr. Gold got all them squatters outa here."

"I thought so, too," I said, although I was no longer very sure myself.

"Well, somethin' isn't right."

"What happened?"

"Someone lit a fire in the apartment next door to mine."

"What?"

"Just a little one, some garbage maybe. I smelled it and put it out with a bucket of water."

"You went into the apartment next door and put a fire out?"

"Well, it was easier than callin' the fire folks. And quicker."

"And more dangerous. Ian, you're eighty years old."

"Don't remind me, darlin'."

"You're sure you got it out?"

"Oh yes. But there's sounds now. There's people around."

I knew what he was asking me. He wanted me to come

and look around. I was Arnold's volunteer assistant, and if the tenants had problems, I was the one to call.

"I'll be there in an hour, Ian."

"I don't want to trouble your Sunday," he said.

No, of course not. "I'm on my way."

It was late Sunday afternoon in October, and the summer stream of weekenders returning to the city had abated. I got to 603 long before an hour had passed, and parked almost in front of it. I took out my flashlight and keys while I was still in the car so that I wouldn't have to open my bag on the street in the dusk. I didn't like coming here at night. I didn't like looking for squatters, who were probably addicts, or any other "folks" who might be inhabiting the building. But I knew that the police had had their fill of calls from 603 and wouldn't give another vague complaint much priority. I went in the first door, unlocked the inner one, and turned on my flashlight.

There were, of course, no light bulbs in the lobby. You didn't notice it that much during the day, but now it was practically dark. I shone my light all around the old marble floor and walls, and saw nothing. I went to the stairwell and pulled the door open. No sound. I flashed my light down toward the basement and up toward the second floor. Nothing as far as the landings. I started up.

You go into things sometimes knowing in your head that they're dangerous, but that silly, childish belief in the invulnerability of the self asserts itself. Whoever this man was—if it was the same one—he had attacked me, assaulted me, followed me home, lit a fire on my lawn, and now lit one in the apartment next door to Gallagher, but I couldn't quite believe he could kill me. I had failed to overpower him when he held me, and still I felt I could come out of an encounter alive. But I was scared.

I got to three and stopped. I turned off the flashlight and listened. If someone was waiting on the stairs, he didn't move. I turned the light back on and opened the door. I didn't hear anything. I walked into the hall. It was quiet.

As quickly as I could, I went to Ian's apartment and rang the bell. There was no answer.

"Ian," I called, remembering that terrible morning when I had stood in front of Nathan's door and called his name. "Ian, are you there?"

No answer.

My first thought was that they had gotten him, too. Something had happened between his call to me and now, something had gotten him out of his apartment again and persuaded him to open his door to a push-in murderer.

If Ian was dead, only Mrs. Paterno would be left in this building, and it was a cinch she wouldn't stay long. Metropolitan would have achieved its goal. They could gut and renovate with two deaths to their credit. Or three if I didn't get out of here fast.

It was still deathly quiet. I turned off my flashlight. I wrapped my left arm around my handbag as I had the other day. I didn't like the feeling of déjà vu; I had lost the last time. Tonight I might lose worse. I steadied myself and made for the stairway.

The shadow glided out of one of the empty apartments the other side of the stairway, and I knew I didn't have a prayer. I was forced into one of the empty apartments, where I would have to play cat and mouse. I darted in the nearest door and, not thinking very clearly, hid right behind it. There wasn't even a doorknob to hang on to. Everything of scrap value had been removed by Metropolitan months or years ago as the apartments had emptied. I was now wedged in a corner behind an open door. To my right along the wall was the same kind of long hall that everyone else's apartment started with. I didn't want to chance going into one of the rooms, because it was too easy to be cornered there. So I was cornered here. Literally.

I listened for him. He was probably wearing sneakers, as I was, and he wasn't in any hurry. Why should he be? He had me.

But who was it? Jesus Ramirez was safely behind bars. Did Metropolitan have a whole stable of thugs and killers? Or was this a squatter who wanted the whole building for himself? Or someone after me personally? And if so, would he have killed Ian? There were too many questions and not enough answers.

I didn't have much time to ponder. There was a sound in the outside hall, and I knew he was coming to get me. Even so, I felt revulsion at having to lean against this filthy, roach-infested wall. Something soft touched my neck, and I reached reflexively to rid myself of it, not caring whether it was a cobweb or a living thing, or whether I made a noise that gave me away. I was absolutely terrified.

When he stepped over the threshold, I was ready for him. I pushed the door with as much speed and force as I could generate. He made a sound, stepped back, and I pulled the door open and braced myself for a second charge. It came in seconds. Those are heavy doors on those old apartments, fire doors made with metal to last forever. You get hit with it, you get hurt.

He got hurt. I heard him grunt and fall. I pulled the door open and edged out of my hiding place so that I could escape, and I almost tripped over his body. I stepped over him as he began to move, and for safe measure, hit him on the side of the head with my flashlight. Then I started running.

I could have hit him harder. One of the toughest things to do is to hurt another human being, and the closer you come to direct contact, the harder it is. I understood in that moment as I fled for my life the awful appeal of guns. You can stand a safe distance from your enemy and use your index finger on a piece of cold metal to inflict pain or even death. You're one giant step removed from the deed. Hitting someone with an object in your hand, or, God forbid, plunging a knife into another person's body, is tough. So I didn't hit him as hard as I could have, and I wasn't surprised when I heard him take off after me.

But I was safely in the stairwell, safely ahead of him, safely on my way to the lobby and freedom. Except that when I got to the first floor, the door to the lobby wouldn't open. I was sure as I tried the doorknob and pushed over and over that I was just not doing it right, but after several quick tries in each direction, I gave up. Going back upstairs was out of the question. He was on my tail.

I had no choice but to go down to the basement.

I will tell you that I was as near hysterics at that moment as I ever get. Any feeling of invulnerability had left me when Ian didn't answer his door. I was vulnerable, someone was after me, and he was a killer. And I had hurt him. That meant he was an angry killer.

But the basement harbored rats. I don't know which threat frightened me more, the one above me or the one below. But I had no choice. Going up was suicide. I am a Catholic. I do not commit suicide.

Next to the basement door was a door to the street. I tried it, but it was locked. I pulled open the basement door, dashed inside, and flicked on my flashlight, hearing rustling, scurrying sounds as the light moved. The basement was the size of the whole building. It was also filled with junk as well as the machinery needed to heat the building and make hot water for the tenants.

Across the floor I could see what looked like a row of open gates or doors. I flashed my light ahead of me to scare away whatever else occupied the basement and started for the bins, hearing those terrifying sounds as I moved. Probably those enclosures were where the tenants stored things like luggage and old furniture, if they had the guts to come down here. There were so many of them that if I hid in one, it would give me time to think, maybe to get away if my assailant was in another part of the basement. I didn't get there. I heard him approach the door and I turned my light off. It was so dark that he wouldn't see me if I crouched behind some junk and kept still. I didn't know whether there were lights down here, or if there were, if he knew where the switches were. In the meantime, if he went in the other direction, I might be able to move toward a storage bin.

He shuffled around in the dark, never saying anything. I heard something fall at the other end of the basement, and I crept carefully away from this pile of junk and toward another that was closer to the line of bins. I was sure he hadn't heard me. But as I settled into my new hiding place, something grazed my ankle, something living, something slightly warm, and I could not keep myself from whimpering, although I held a hand over my mouth.

I still couldn't see him, although my eyes had gotten about as used to the dark as they would get. Around three-quarters of the perimeter of the basement were small windows high up through which almost no light entered. I guessed that the wall without windows faced the street, where streetlights might have provided a little light. The windows were probably inside wells anyway, and it was dark out by now.

I took a chance and moved again. There were sounds, but not too close. I moved a little farther. Then I felt something solid against my back. I turned and touched the wall gingerly. It was wooden slats. I had reached the bins.

I crept along the slatted wall till I came to an opening, then eased myself in. The scurrying inside was unmistakable. I was so terrified that I froze. I knew that rats bit and that they carried unmentionable diseases. I worked to stay calm because I had to. This was my show. Nobody except Gallagher knew I was coming here tonight, and Gallagher was probably dead. I could have called Jack, but I didn't. I could have called Arnold. I hadn't. I was now completely responsible for saving my own life. I couldn't give in to a hysterical breakdown. It would be fatal.

I stuck my right hand in my pocket and felt something. All of a sudden I knew I had a weapon.

The thought lifted me out of my despair. In my handbag, besides the flashlight and all the other things most women carry, I kept a roll of quarters. Quarters fed the parking meters on Broadway. Quarters fed the phones. In a single day I might use five or ten of them, once upon a time my daily allowance. So I kept a roll handy in case I ran out.

In my pocket I had felt the silky fabric of one of Aunt Meg's beautiful scarves. I had used it once in the rain, stuffed it in the pocket, and left it there. Without moving my feet toward the other occupants of the bin, I opened my bag silently and felt around for the roll of quarters. I took it out and hefted it. It would do nicely. I placed it in the center of the silk scarf, gathered the four corners, and knotted them. Then, holding the loose ends, I swung the scarf so that the weighted center made circles in the air. I had myself a sap.

I moved carefully to the open bin door and waited just behind it. I've always thought that the defenders of those old forts had the advantage over the Indians in time of attack. Now I was a defender. I had a weapon and I would use it.

He kept stumbling on things, so I knew he didn't have a flashlight or didn't want to use it. He never turned on the basement lights. I just waited, holding the silk scarf, trying not to think of the rats' nest only a few feet from where I stood. Sooner or later he would start trying the doors to the bins.

It was sooner. I heard the squeal of hinges to my left, then another squeal a little closer. I heard him whisper something, probably an obscenity or a string of them, but I couldn't make out the words. Then I heard his footsteps get closer. The slatted door moved just a little. A dark figure passed about a foot beyond the door.

I lifted the sap and swung it for all I was worth. Contact!

He shouted, "Ow!" and brought his hand up to his head. I swung again.

This time he went down. I stepped on top of him to get out, turned on the flashlight, which I'd been holding in my other hand, and ran for the door. Before going up the stairs to one, I tried the outside door at the basement level once again. It opened easily and I went out into the cool night, up the stairs, around the building through the alley to the street and up toward Broadway.

I didn't get there. A police car appeared miraculously as I reached West End. I hailed it, told my story in rapid bursts as I tried to catch my breath, got in, and directed them to 603. We all flew out of the car and ran for the front door. I unlocked the inside door, and the policemen charged ahead for the stairwell. The door, of course, opened easily and down they went, calling to me to stay behind. As I leaned against the wall, Ian Gallagher walked in the front door.

* * *

They never found him, of course. One of the policemen said I probably hadn't hit him very hard. Eventually I went down and showed them where I thought I'd been hiding. Yes, there was evidence of a rats' nest, a lot of footprints in the dust, and even something on the filthy floor that might have been a fresh bloodstain. But the man was gone.

As for Ian, he had suddenly remembered that he needed some cornflakes or something for breakfast and had hurried out before the neighborhood bodega closed. ("An' you said an hour, darlin', so I thought you meant a little more.")

I gave another statement to the police, kissed Ian good night, and drove home. My jeans weren't new and stiff anymore. I'd broken them in good.

18

I skipped my walk on Monday morning and very nearly skipped breakfast. I don't have to tell you I hadn't slept well and I was a pack of nerves. No one besides Bettina knew what was going on, but I felt if I told either Arnold or Jack, they'd come and get me to prevent me from going through with it. I half hoped Jack would call, as he often did, before leaving for work so that I could break down and tell him what had happened last night and what I was doing this afternoon. But no one called, and the morning dragged on.

At five after ten I called Franciotti's number. He wasn't there. He would be in soon. But I couldn't wait.

I left a fairly detailed message with the officer who answered. I gave him my name and Bettina's name and address, the time of our meeting, and the fact that someone was coming there who might have killed Nathan Herskovitz.

"I think they arrested a suspect in that case," the officer said politely.

"But it may have been the wrong one. Look, I'll call Sergeant Franciotti back about eleven or a little after. I'll be on the road till then. Will you see to it that he's available?"

"I can't promise, ma'am. If something comes up, he—"

"Officer, the man I'm meeting may be a killer. You can't tell me maybe."

"I'll give the message to the sergeant," the officer said noncommittally.

"Thank you."

I left the house feeling apprehensive. I was getting myself into another mess, and what was worse, getting an old woman

152

into the same mess. If anything happened to her, I would never forgive myself—if I survived.

I arrived in the Seventies at ten to eleven, ten minutes before the parking restrictions went off north of Seventy-second Street. I drove to Seventy-third, where there were still a few spots on the new good side (they start parking there half an hour early and sit in their cars till eleven) and lots of spaces on the new bad side. The bad side would do me fine. It was good till eight tomorrow morning, and assuming I was alive later today, I had no intention of staying overnight.

I walked down to Seventy-second and over to Bettina's building. She buzzed me in and I went upstairs.

"So when do the police come?" was the first thing she asked.

"I haven't been able to reach Sergeant Franciotti," I told her honestly. "I'd like to call him now."

"In the kitchen."

I called the precinct and asked for him. He had been in earlier, but he was gone. They didn't know when he would return, but they'd be glad to take a message.

"I've been leaving messages since yesterday," I burst out in a rather uncharacteristically loud and angry voice. "It hasn't done much good. I need him at this address before two o'clock this afternoon. It may be a matter of life and death."

Whoever I was talking to asked for the details. I spelled them out again. He said he'd get a message to Franciotti, but I had the feeling he thought I was nuts.

"And please," I finished, "I don't want a police car parked outside the building with its lights going."

"Sergeant Franciotti drives an unmarked vehicle," the officer said in a monotone.

I hung up.

"You didn't get him?"

"He's been in and now he's out. Bettina, I can't let you stay here with me if there's going to be trouble and I can't get the police. If he doesn't call back and I can't reach him, here's what we'll do."

I had given it some thought on the drive from Oakwood. At a quarter to two Bettina would go to someone's apartment in the building—I thought she must have a friend here, having lived here so long—or out to a nearby coffee shop. At two she would call the 911 number and say there was a robbery in progress and give her address. I figured they'd have to respond to that. If Franciotti was too busy doing other things, someone else could make the collar. (That's what Jack would say; I still think of it as an arrest.)

Bettina agreed, but I sensed she was disappointed. There was a woman down the hall she was friendly with and who was likely to be home. Just to be sure, I had her call. There was no problem with two o'clock.

"Where's the book?" I asked.

"You want to show it to him?"

"I think I have to. If he doesn't see it, he's likely to smell a trap and run."

"I'll get it."

She came back and laid it in my hands. It was really too precious to fool around with, but I had no choice. What a collection Nathan must have had if this was only one of many.

"It's so beautiful," Bettina said, admiring it. "It was one of his best."

Something in her face struck me. "Was it you?" I asked.

She looked confused. "Was what me?"

"Are you the one he was in love with?"

She blushed, then laughed. "You have quite an imagination. No, he wasn't in love with me. We had no affair. I was my husband's wife, with no regrets."

"I'm sorry."

"It's all right. You're looking for something. Maybe we'll find it this afternoon."

She put together a beautiful lunch with several salads and smoked fishes. I was too nervous to eat, which she guessed as I picked at everything. She promised to wrap it all up and give it to me to take home.

I called the precinct twice more with no luck and decided we would have to go with our alternate plan.

"What's my name?" I said to her.

"What?"

"I'm your daughter."

"Rita Cohen," she said instantly. "Tell him Mrs. Cohen. He doesn't have to know your first name."

I actually laughed. During my years in the convent, I was known only by my first name, and since my vows, by my first two, Sister Edward Frances, after both my parents. Now, suddenly, I was going formal with a suspected killer.

"I don't have a wedding ring," I said.

"Wait." She went into the back of the apartment and came back with a gold signet-type ring. "Wear it backward. He'll never know."

I put it on. It was a little big, but it would do. "That's good. Would you write down the address and phone number of where you'll be and leave it for me?"

She wrote on a piece of notepaper and went into the kitchen. "Under the napkin holder," she said, returning. "What else can I do?"

"Just remember the number 911."

"I will. I'll watch from Mrs. Hauser's door. When I see him get off the elevator, I'll call."

"Good. Now I have to think of a place to put that book."

"Maybe in the bedroom."

"No. I don't want him following me, and I don't want to leave him alone in this room."

We looked around the living room silently. Not the piano. Not the piano bench. Not under the seat cushions. There were shelves of records near the stereo and filled bookcases on the walls. Nothing seemed right.

Finally I said, "I think I'll just put it under the sofa."

"That's good."

I lifted the skirt and laid the book on the bare floor. I looked at my watch. It was one-thirty.

"Maybe you ought to go," I said.

"Patience. The doorbell didn't ring yet, did it?"

"Can you fix the door so it'll close and not lock?"

"All you do is press the little button." She showed me.

"Good. Leave it that way. When he comes, I'll turn the bolt to open it, but I won't turn it when I close the door. That way, the police can get in by turning the handle."

"You've thought of everything. I can't see how this can fail."

It can fail if he decides to take the book and kill me, I thought. I lose my life, she loses her book, and no one has Nathan's killer.

"When he rings," I said finally, "I'll call you at Mrs. What's-her-name's."

"Mrs. Hauser. I'll answer the phone."

"Bettina, I think you should go. He might get in downstairs with a tenant, and then I won't know he's here till he's at the door."

She came over and kissed me. "Don't worry so much. It's all under control. I'll watch from the door, you'll call, we'll get him."

"I hope you're right."

She smiled and left the apartment.

19

You know what an eternity is. It's the time it takes for something terrible to happen—or something wonderful. I wear a very inexpensive, very accurate watch powered by a battery. It's the closest thing I have to jewelry, but I wear it because it tells me the time. Two o'clock came and went. I had a near hysterical thought that maybe the book man couldn't find a place to park and had to give up the whole thing.

Then the downstairs bell rang. I went to the kitchen, pressed the speak button, and called, "Who is it?"

The answer was garbled, but I was pretty sure he said, "The book man."

I pressed the buzzer. When I was sure he'd had time to get through the door, I found Bettina's note and dialed the number.

She answered on the first ring.

"He's on his way up," I said.

"Don't worry. As soon as I see him, I'll call the police."

I hung up. Should she have waited? What if he came in and tied me up and found the book and ran before the police got here?

"Steady, Kix," I said out loud. "You are a calm person. You can handle anything."

I was an idiot. I was endangering both my life and a precious book.

Down the outside hall I could hear the elevator door open and close. This was it. I checked my "wedding ring" and stood in the middle of the living room, waiting.

I heard a man's voice outside and wondered fleetingly who he was talking to. Then the doorbell rang.

"Who is it?" I called, feeling ridiculous.

"It's me." The voice was deep.

I opened the door. A stoutish man with thinning, graying hair, dressed in a suit, walked in. Behind him was a younger, shorter, man with dark, unkempt hair and a day's growth of beard. He was dressed in a leather jacket and jeans.

"Who's he?" I asked.

"My helper."

"He's not coming in." I tried to close the door on him, with less success than last night.

"Yes he is." The book man pushed the door open, dislodging me, and the helper came in and slammed it. "You're not the woman I talked to."

"I'm her daughter."

"Where's Mrs. Strauss?"

"She's out for the afternoon."

"I don't like this. Where's the book?"

"Do you have the money to pay for it?"

The book man smiled. "First I look at the book. Then you tell me how much you want for it. Then we arrive at a price. Then you see the money. That's how business is done."

I hadn't gone to his business school. "I want to see that you have money with you. Show it to me." I was starting to be afraid that the whole transaction would last three minutes and they'd be long gone if and when the police showed up.

The book man pulled a wallet out of his jacket pocket as the helper prowled around, casing the room. He opened it and riffled through the wad of bills in it. "Good enough?"

"That's fine."

"Let me see the book."

I had stalled about as long as I dared. I walked over to the sofa, knelt down, and started to reach under the skirt.

"What are you doing there?" the book man said with agitation. "Get her."

The smaller man flew at me, knocking me over roughly

so that I banged my head on the floor, and held me down so that I couldn't move.

"Let her go," the book man said, "but watch her. See what's under the couch."

He released me, and I pulled myself along the floor away from him. His hands were filthy, and he smelled.

"Be careful!" I shouted as he reached under the sofa skirt. "That's a very valuable book."

"She's right," the book man said.

"Here it is." The helper picked it up, got up, and handed it to the book man.

The book man's eyes widened. His whole face changed, softened. He licked his lips. He held the volume as though it were a fragile piece of crystal. His head started nodding.

I stayed on the floor, watching the helper, who was watching me. He was rough and hard-looking with dark, threatening eyes, the kind of guy you don't want to run into in the proverbial dark alley.

"How much you want for it?" the book man asked.

"Ten thousand dollars," I said. I had decided on the price earlier. I had no idea whether the book was worth hundreds, thousands, or more.

"I'll give you a thousand for it. That's more than it's worth."

"My mother needs the money. She's old and she has a lot of expenses."

"Eleven hundred."

Where were the police? "It's not enough."

"You tell me where the big one is, I'll give you more."

"The big what?"

"The Herskovitz book. The Guadalaxara."

"I don't know what you're talking about."

"I bet your mother knows. Herskovitz killed a man for that book."

I stared at him. "Leave my mother alone."

That's when the door opened and two uniformed policemen came in, guns drawn. It took a second look for me to see that one of them was female and probably several years younger than I.

"Hold it," the male officer said, and both the book man and his helper stopped dead.

"You all right, ma'am?" the female asked.

"I'm fine." I rubbed the back of my head where it hurt and pulled myself to my feet, feeling a moment of mild dizziness.

Bettina came through the open door calling, "Chris, Chris, are you all right?"

I steadied myself and she hugged me. I was about to say something when Sergeant Franciotti and the other man who had been with him the morning we found Nathan came into the apartment.

"You're late," I said.

"Miss Bennett," he said, articulating my name carefully. "You want to tell me what's going on here?"

"Burglary in progress, Sarge," the uniformed policeman said.

"Not exactly," I said to Franciotti.

The uniformed cops were leading the book man and his helper over to a wall when Bettina said, "Please, not against my wall. I'll never get the smudges off. Could you do it against the door?"

"Yes, ma'am," the policeman said, rolling his eyes.

The two suspects leaned against the door while they were patted down. The helper had a gun. Seeing it gave me a chill.

Franciotti looked at the suspects again. "So, Jesus sweetheart, we meet again. Who the hell bailed you out?"

The helper nodded his head at the book man. "He did."

"Is this—is he Ramirez?" I asked incredulously.

"You got it," Franciotti said, gloating.

"Oh no."

"Oh yes, Miss Bennett."

The policewoman started reading the Miranda warnings. I listened, fascinated, as though I had never heard the words before.

"Who's the other one?" I asked, still trying to make sense out of Ramirez's presence here.

"The suit?" the policeman said. He looked at something he had in his hand. "Warren Finch."

"Finch," I said. The name rang a bell. Finch, Finch, *Finch*. I had seen it somewhere, read it somewhere. "Metropolitan Properties," I blurted. "He owns the building Nathan Herskovitz was murdered in."

Franciotti looked at me. "You sure?"

Before I could answer, the book man said, "That's my brothers. I don't own real estate."

"But it gives him access to the building, doesn't it?" I said, trying to think it through. Then I shook my head. "It still doesn't work. Ramirez was in jail Wednesday night when Nathan's apartment was broken into."

"How's your little brother, Jesus?" Franciotti said. "Angel still doin' odd jobs for Metropolitan?"

"I wan' my lawyer," Ramirez said. "I din' kill no one."

Angel and Jesus, I thought. What had their poor mother been thinking? "If you pick up Angel," I said to Franciotti, "see if he has a bump on his head."

Franciotti turned to me. "You want to explain what's going on here?"

"I think I'd better."

"Take 'em away," his partner told the uniforms. Franciotti sat down on the sofa and pulled out his spiral notebook and a ballpoint pen. I heard it click into position.

"I could give you a lovely lunch," Bettina said.

"Oh, that's very nice of you, ma'am, but we just ate."

Right, I thought, just what Jack always says. Get yourself a meal before you answer a call. You never know when you'll get the next one.

I sat down and told him the whole story.

20

I took a hot bath when I got home. Then I unwrapped the little packages Bettina had sent home with me. I must have eaten two pounds of food before I gave up and washed the dishes.

I wanted to strangle Arnold. He had actually gotten the judge to set bail, and Warren Finch had had the money to get Jesus out. I had the kinds of thoughts that would have sent me to confession a year ago. Now I just thought of them as letting off steam.

Franciotti had taken a lot of time getting my statement. At some point he made a phone call to have Ramirez's brother, Angel, picked up.

I told Franciotti everything that I thought was pertinent to the murder, including what had happened last night, except my feeble suspicion of Mrs. Paterno. I told him about Nathan and the books.

"How'd you find out all this stuff?" he asked.

"I talked to the people who went to the funeral."

"I see."

He wasn't happy about last night or our little afternoon caper, but I pointed out that I had called him about half a dozen times, leaving very explicit messages, none of which he had answered. He apologized. Anyway, the case was closed.

It was Arnold who called me. He didn't know I'd been involved in the afternoon's activities, but he wanted to keep me up-to-date on Ramirez. He listened to my story, scolded me gently—Arnold does know how to be gentle—and said as far as he was concerned, we still didn't have Nathan's killer.

"Come on, Arnold," I said wearily. "Ramirez was carrying a gun."

"Everyone in New York carries a gun. Don't you carry one?"

"No, and you don't either."

"But I'm a maverick. Listen, Chrissie, in plain English, Ramirez is a no-good bum. He's not a hired killer. And Nathan wasn't killed with a gun, remember? I have evidence that says Ramirez wasn't in Manhattan, wasn't anywhere in New York last Friday or Saturday."

"Are you serious?"

"He was in Puerto Rico visiting his sick mother."

"I don't believe this."

"I've got a good case."

"Maybe his brother did it."

"I can't vouch for his brother," Arnold said. "I'm just telling you, the case isn't closed."

It was for me. One Ramirez was the same as another. The only connection I could see between Nathan's book and his murder was that Warren Finch had seen the murder as a chance to move in on the collection. I had told Franciotti to talk to Mr. McCandless at the auction house, just to see whether Finch was one of the interested parties who had called.

I still had many questions about Nathan's life, but unless they connected to his murder, they constituted prying. They would have to go unanswered.

When the phone rang, I expected Melanie Gross, or maybe Bettina checking up on me, but what I got was a wonderful surprise.

"Chris? This is Angela at St. Stephen's. I have Joseph on the phone for you."

My heart leaped up, to paraphrase Wordsworth. Joseph is the General Superior of St. Stephen's, once called the Mother Superior, but no longer. But more than that, she was my spiritual director for all the years I was at St. Stephen's, and my closest friend, although she is at least fifteen years older than I. I had not seen or spoken to her since July, and I cannot describe how happy I was that she was calling. I said a few words to Sister Angela, and then she put me through.

"Chris, how are you?"

"Fine, happy. It's wonderful to hear your voice."

"Well, if you're free tomorrow afternoon, you can see me in person."

"I am."

"I have a meeting at the Chancery in the morning. Can you be at Celia's apartment about two?"

"Easily. The class I teach is over at eleven-thirty."

"Good. If I'm not there yet, wait in the lobby. I have the key."

We spoke for another minute, then hung up. Joseph would listen. Joseph would understand better than anyone else.

When the phone rang next, it was Mark Brownstein asking if I was free on Saturday.

"Mark," I said, "I've been so tied up in this murder that happened on Yom Kippur that I feel all swallowed up."

"I know you're never home. I've tried you almost every day around lunchtime."

"I don't remember the last time I ate lunch at home. I'm afraid this week is out. You know, I still have your prayer book. I'm going to be in the city Saturday afternoon. If I have the time, I'll leave it with your doorman."

"Don't worry about it. It's another year to Yom Kippur."

"Would you mind if I called you when I come out from under?"

"I'll look forward to it."

I had a feeling he meant it. I sat down with the paper, but my mind wouldn't let me concentrate. Could Warren Finch have killed Nathan himself? He was obviously the mysterious caller who was bothering Nathan. Could he have waited for him at his apartment, gone in, and killed him when Nathan refused to turn over the book to him?

I didn't know. Somehow it didn't seem likely. A paunchy older man who went to meet two women and brought along an armed "helper" wasn't the type to do it himself. And how could he have walked out splattered with blood? Maybe it had been Jesus's brother. I was too tired to think about it anymore.

I was already asleep when the phone rang at ten o'clock, and I had to drag myself out of that sleep to answer.

"Anything you want to tell me?"

It was Jack, sounding like his old self.

"About what?" I asked cagily.

"Oh, about that tea party you had this afternoon."

"How could you possibly know about that?"

"I'm just keeping track of Ramirez and company. Sounds like you gave Franciotti quite a statement."

I laughed. We talked. He kidded me after he told me how dangerous what I'd done was. I liked the way he sounded. Caring.

"How'd it go tonight?" I asked finally.

"It's OK. I'm sorry about Saturday."

I felt confused. "Can't you make it?"

"I mean last Saturday. I shouldn't talk to real human beings when I feel that way."

"Everything OK at school?"

"I got it together over the weekend. It was different, and I panicked and shouldn't have. Something just clicked yesterday."

I felt as good as if it had happened to me. "I'm glad."

"We set for Saturday?"

"Yes. I'll go down to Nathan's in the afternoon to see Mitchell and his wife, give them a hand if they need it."

"What's the apartment number?"

"It's 5D. Be careful on the stairs. Jack, do you think this man Finch could have killed Nathan?"

"Sounds gutless to me."

"He is."

"I'll see you in Manhattan on Saturday."

"Good night."

I hope he slept as well as I did.

21

My poetry class got a little hairy. It was the first poetry class I've ever attended that included a shouting match.

"Sentimental!" Carson, one of my big talkers, called over and over as lines were quoted.

"Bullshit," someone retorted from the other side of the room.

"Is any poetry free of sentimentality?" I asked.

"Sure," Carson said.

"Read me half a dozen consecutive lines."

She looked around the room. " 'When in the Course of human Events, it becomes necessary for one People to—' "

"That's not poetry," Morgan interrupted, "it's the Constitution."

"It's the Declaration of Independence," I said. "The Constitution starts, 'We the people of the United States.' "

Morgan looked miffed. "It's still not poetry."

"It sounds like poetry," Carson said.

"Does that make it poetry?" I asked.

They fought about it for a while.

"I think we lost sentimentality," I reminded them a few minutes later. "Anyone want to define it?"

They eventually decided that "gushy" was the best definition. "Where does love fit in?" I asked. "And death? And pity?"

"I've got it," Carson said. "If it's about love, it's sentimental. If it's about sex, it's not."

"You mean if he writes to his coy mistress, that's poetry,

and if he writes to a woman he worships from, let's say afar, that's sentimental trash."

"Yes," Carson said as though she had had a revelation. "Yes. That's exactly right."

A few clustered around my desk when the class was over, and we continued to talk. They were ten or twelve years younger than I, and some of them probably dated men my age, but they seemed like such children, exciting, delightful children, but children nevertheless. Two of them walked me to the parking lot and lingered a moment at my car. Maybe next week I would have lunch with them. They were my window to the world I had only recently entered.

I got into New York in good time, parked on Broadway near Seventy-ninth Street, and fed a quarter into the meter, breaking open the roll that had saved my life. I hadn't seen Gallagher since our brief meeting Sunday night, and I wanted to talk to him, even if it meant missing lunch. Celia would probably have left a bite to eat in her apartment for Joseph and me.

Gallagher was home. He came to the door wearing the usual heavy brown sweater and a pair of worn corduroys.

"How's my girl?" he asked as I came in.

"Pretty good, Ian. Do you have a minute?"

"For you? A minute and then some."

We went into his living room and sat down. "Ian, if I can make a decent arrangement, are you willing to move out of here?"

"I've been willing all along. I told you, I can't afford what's out there."

"Maybe you can. May I use your phone?"

"Be my guest."

I wanted him to hear the conversation. I dialed Metropolitan Properties and asked for Bertram Finch.

"He's in conference," the secretary said. It's what she always said.

"Tell him it's Christine Bennett, Arnold Gold's assistant, and I must speak to him."

"Just a minute."

It took less than that for Bertram Finch to come on the line. "Miss Bennett. What can I do for you?"

"Mr. Finch, I've been talking to your tenants at 603. Both Mrs. Paterno and Mr. Gallagher are agreed that they would like to vacate their apartments if you can find them equivalent apartments on the West Side." I knew Metropolitan owned several buildings in the area, and the rumor was that they were "warehousing" apartments, keeping them empty till they could get them off rent control and rent them for much more money. "Here's what they're willing to agree to. They'll pay up to ten dollars a month more in rent." (I heard him groan. Both Paterno and Gallagher were paying rents typical of those charged a quarter century ago.) "They want all their moving expenses paid. They want a guarantee of no rent increases for the rest of their lives. And they want a bonus of ten thousand dollars apiece." I saw Gallagher's eyes bulge as he heard this last. "Arnold Gold can draw up the papers."

"I don't know if I can—"

"How is your brother Warren, Mr. Finch?"

I heard him breathe. "That was you, wasn't it?" he asked.

"It certainly was."

"My brother only wanted to buy a book."

"I'll probably be called to testify," I said. "And I'm sure you know I was assaulted in 603 on Sunday night."

"I don't know anything about that," he said crisply. Then, in a different voice, "Look—Miss Bennett—I'll see what I can do."

"That's all I ask."

"Did he go for it?" Ian asked when I got off the phone.

"He's giving it a lot of thought, Ian. Did I say anything I shouldn't have?"

"God bless you, girl. I wouldn't have cut a single word."

Joseph was already in Celia's apartment when I got there, and I smelled coffee brewing as she opened the door. We greeted each other warmly and sat talking over coffee and lovely little cakes that Celia had indeed left for us. Joseph is a tall, handsome woman. She is bright and sharp and compassionate. I have known her and loved her since that terrible night fifteen years ago when Aunt Meg left me at St. Stephen's amid tears and recriminations. I went from child to adult under Joseph's watchful eye, and she has been a source of strength to me when I needed one.

She was serving her first elected term as General Superior, and I expected her to be elected to a second term when this one was through.

When we had finished our gossiping, she asked me how I was coming and what I was doing. They were questions I had hoped she would ask.

"I need to talk to you," I said. "I've become involved in a murder investigation."

From the look on her face, she seemed to be both pleased and interested. "Let's sit in the living room," she said. "And tell me all about it."

I told her much more than I had told Franciotti. I included my feeling that Nathan had had an affair in the fifties, and I told her about Amelia Paterno. In fact, I told her everything, including what had happened yesterday at Bettina Strauss's. When it seemed that I might be skipping over details, she stopped me and asked me not to rush. All I omitted was Jack and my relationship with him, a part of my life that I now considered supremely private.

When I finished, she sat very still, not looking at me, not looking at anything. Finally she said, "I'm interested in what you chose to tell me and what you chose not to tell me."

"I told you everything. I can't think of one thing I've left out."

"They were all facts, Chris. You related events. This happened, then that happened, then something else. I felt as though you were reading your notebook to me. You're very good at description. I can see that bloody apartment in that vacant, rat-infested building. I love that little man, Greenspan, who counts the sunsets he watches in his old age and answers questions with questions of his own. And of course, that's all necessary to understand the situation, but you've left out the most important part. You never said one word about how you feel about Mr. Herskovitz.''

''I loved him, Joseph.'' It was the first time I had ever said it, and the first time I had thought about it, the first time I had really known it. Hearing my own words, I knew it was true. I felt tears come to my eyes.

''Yes,'' Joseph said with satisfaction. ''And why did you love him?''

''He talked to me. Not the way Gallagher does with his complaints and his stories about the way things used to be, over and over. Nathan conversed, he asked questions, he listened. I learned from him, and I think he learned from me. I found books in his night table that I had recommended. I guess in some ways he was the perfect grandfather, and I was the perfect granddaughter. We weren't related, there were no ties between us, and we owed each other nothing. When we spent time together, it was because we wanted to.''

''I begin to see him now,'' Joseph said. ''Tell me, how do you feel about his relationship with Mrs. Paterno?''

''If it started after his wife died, it doesn't bother me at all. If it went on while she was alive, it troubles me.''

''Do you intend to tell his children about his relationship with Mrs. Paterno?''

''No. I don't see any need to. It really isn't their business.''

''Exactly. Was his first family their business?''

''I don't know.''

''In other words, two intelligent people might have differing opinions on that, and we might find something in both points of view to agree with.''

''Very likely.''

''Think about it, Chris. We're not talking about truths and untruths; we're talking about discretion. Perhaps you've been asking all the right questions but about the wrong person.''

I stared at her, and suddenly it all made sense.

22

I tried Bettina's number before I left Celia's apartment, but there was no answer. I left a note for Celia that I wanted to stay over on Saturday night, and then Joseph and I left, Joseph to get a taxi to Grand Central, I to ransom my car from a very expensive parking garage.

On Wednesday morning I called Bettina and asked if I might come in and talk to her. I had forgotten to give her back my "wedding ring," but it was more than that; there are things I can't say on the telephone. I needed to see her face-to-face.

I got down to the area by ten, an awkward time to find a space. I wove in and out of streets, one way in this direction, the other way in that, with no luck. I didn't want to park on Broadway because I'd have to come back in an hour and feed the meter. It was one pressure I could do without today.

I went over to Riverside Drive and Eighty-first and drove slowly south. Just below Seventy-ninth a small car was pulling out, and I got the space. It would be a healthy walk to Bettina's, but a walk has never daunted me.

I locked the car and started south. Across the street, in front of an apartment house, an ambulance stood at the curb. As I approached it, I started to get an uncomfortable feeling.

It was standing in front of Mr. Greenspan's building. That gave me more than a chill. I crossed the street and started running. A dog walker and a couple of women were standing in front of the building. There was no one in the ambulance.

"Do you know who it is?" I asked, addressing all of them.

"Nah," the dog walker said. "They should be bringing him down pretty soon. They've been here a while."

The women looked at me but said nothing.

I stood watching the glass doors. Finally I saw them, two attendants and a stretcher on wheels. The dog walker and one of the women got to the doors before me, opened them, and held them.

The attendants pulled the stretcher out onto the sidewalk and left it while they went to the ambulance. Feeling a little queasy, I walked closer to see who it was wrapped in all that linen.

Two familiar bright eyes peered at me.

"Mr. Greenspan," I said.

"You."

"Yes, it's me, Chris."

"I know who you are. You're too early."

"For what?"

"For the sunset. It's still morning."

I forced a smile. "I'll come back next week. Is that all right?"

"Next week is fine. I'll be home. It's just a little pain. They think it's a heart attack, but it's not, and nobody listens to me. What do they know? Listen, the murderer. He didn't call back."

The crew returned, and one of them asked me to leave. They started moving the stretcher to the open back of the ambulance.

"It's all right, Mr. Greenspan," I said, walking beside them, to the annoyance of the self-important nearer crew member. "We got him. Yesterday afternoon. You have nothing to worry about."

The last I saw of him was a big smile.

I waited till the ambulance drove off. It was from St. Luke's, and I made a note to call. Then I walked down toward Seventy-second Street with a heavy heart. I hoped they would give him a room facing west.

* * *

Bettina refused to take the ring back. "It's too small for me," she said. "You it fits perfectly. It's a nice ring. You should wear a little gold."

"Thank you."

"Did we get the two that killed Nathan?"

"I don't know. The little man, Ramirez, may not even have been in New York that day. And I can hardly imagine the book man doing something like that himself."

"So it was for nothing?"

"It isn't very clear yet. The book man may have been behind the murder, even if he didn't do it himself. And he must have had someone break into Nathan's apartment last week to steal the address book. I'll call Sergeant Franciotti later and see if he's found out anything."

I told her about Mr. Greenspan, and she called the hospital, but he hadn't even cleared the emergency room yet. She looked genuinely worried, and I assured her he was in excellent spirits.

Eventually I had to come to the point of my visit. "I asked you a lot of questions," I said, "and I think you were honest with me."

"I was." She smiled.

"I have another one." I didn't smile. I felt tense and excited and a little nervous. "You knew Hannah Herskovitz?"

"We all knew each other."

"Was Hannah involved with another man before her death?"

I thought I heard a little moan from her. She wasn't smiling anymore. "I learned a long time ago, you only answer the question they ask you. You never add anything. It just gets you in trouble. How did you know about Hannah?"

"I didn't." But I knew it now, and I could feel my skin tingling. "Did Nathan know?"

"He must have. Yes, Nathan knew. He was no fool."

"He must have been devastated." I threw it out and waited.

"He was." Her voice was faltering. She had shared his pain.

''Did it go on for long?''

''Long enough.''

''She was younger than Nathan, wasn't she?''

''A little.'' She said it grudgingly.

''Ten years? Twenty?''

She nodded. ''Fifteen, sixteen, I don't know.''

''Maybe that was the reason, Bettina,'' I said softly.

''Age isn't a reason for doing what she did. He was such a good man, a handsome man, a generous, kind person. He loved her, you know.''

''I know.''

''It's why he never told the children.''

''He let his daughter hate him so that he wouldn't have to tell her the truth about her mother.''

Bettina nodded. She was weeping now. ''The only thing, he couldn't bring himself to go to her funeral.''

I took her out for lunch. After a while she was able to talk about it calmly. Hannah's death had pretty much ended the circle. Nathan wouldn't attend anymore, and small dissensions had arisen. The good friendships remained, but the big, happy get-togethers were over.

I wanted to know who it was. Having come this far, I felt I needed to know everything. She would not tell me. At first she pretended not to know. When it became clear that she did, she just said it was the past and no good could be served by telling me. I walked her back to her apartment house and left her.

Passing Mr. Greenspan's building, I decided to drive up to St. Luke's and inquire about him. Maybe they would let me visit.

I found a meter on Amsterdam Avenue above 110th Street and walked up to the hospital. The woman at the desk had some trouble finding his name, which scared me, but she did finally and said he was in stable condition but could not have visitors today. I left a message for him, which she promised to deliver.

I went back to the car and drove to Broadway. There was an entrance to the highway at 125th Street, which I had never used but which I would now try to find. I turned right on Broadway and started uptown. There were college kids in the streets and collegey-type shops on Broadway. Columbia covered a huge section from 114th up to 120th. At least one of the mourners at Nathan's funeral lived up here. I pulled over to the curb next to a hydrant and took out my list. Weiss, Professor and Mrs. Herbert. The address was Claremont Avenue, which my map had shown as a street only a few blocks long between Broadway and Riverside Drive starting at 116th Street. That was just up ahead.

I made a left on 116th and a right on Claremont. University buildings lined the right-hand side of the street, and old apartment houses the left. I found the Weisses' building and parked at another hydrant. Nothing else seemed available.

I sat back, considering. What would I ask them? I knew about the books now, I knew about Professor Black's deception, I knew about Hannah's infidelity. If Nathan had wanted to keep that quiet, I couldn't in good conscience go blathering about it. These people would know or they wouldn't know. What difference would it make?

What I wanted was to know who the man was, to see if he somehow fit into Nathan's murder. Possibly she had met someone who once lived in 603 and had long since moved. I just didn't have the resources to trace all the families who had lived there, and I was not about to interview a bunch of elderly widows to find out whether one of their husbands had had an affair with Hannah Herskovitz thirty-five years ago.

I thought about my delightful friend, Hillel Greenspan. He had said Hannah was sick. That's how you protect someone, isn't it? I thought. Say they're sick. You can even believe it. Anyone who would cheat on Nathan Herskovitz is sick. Anyone who would commit suicide is sick.

He knew, but he wouldn't tell me, and I couldn't ask him, not with his health so precarious. Besides, it was unlikely that he was the man. He was as old as Nathan, give or take a couple of years. Hannah was younger, much younger.

I took my notebook and pencil out of my bag. Suppose she was fifteen to twenty years younger than Nathan. In 1945, when they met, she would have been twenty-two or twenty-three to his forty. Fourteen years later when she committed suicide, she would have been about thirty-six.

I thought momentarily of Zilman and rejected him. He was too disgusting a man for a young, lovely woman to have had an affair with, whatever his age. In the circle no one else would have been the right age at that time. The only other person I knew, H. K. Granite, had told me he had been "fairly young" before the war. It had been his parents whom Nathan had had a friendship with, his parents who had been given one of the Herskovitz books. Granite, still living at home with his folks, had participated in the circle only when it met at his parents' apartment. Hannah was not likely to have had an affair with a kid.

So that was it. Unless I twisted Bettina's arm or provoked a heart attack in Hillel Greenspan, I had come to the end of my search.

There was a knock on my car window, and I jumped, startled. A blue uniform stood next to my car, and in my side-view mirror I could see a blue-and-white car double-parked just behind me. I rolled the window down.

"I'm afraid you'll have to move your car. You're parked next to a hydrant," the policeman said.

"I'm sorry, Officer. I was just thinking."

I could feel him judging my sanity. "Somewhere else, please," he said.

"OK." I rolled the window back up and started the motor. After a long block, I came to a cross street and turned left. One more block and I was on Riverside Drive. I drove north, toward home. Up ahead was Grant's Tomb.

I went slowly, still trying to figure it out. Nathan was eighty-five, Granite was seventy, Hannah . . . Granite was seventy. If he was seventy, he was fifteen years younger than Nathan. But Hannah was fifteen to twenty years younger than Nathan. That meant they were the same age or Hannah was a little younger than he.

Then what had he meant about being a youngster before the war? I thought suddenly about my students, eighteen-

and nineteen-year-olds who yesterday morning had seemed so young compared to me, and I was only thirty. Of course he was a youngster before the war. He was eighteen or nineteen years old!

At the north end of Grant's Tomb, which sits on an island in the middle of Riverside Drive, you can elect to continue north or swing around the island and go back south. I made the swing, drove back to 116th Street, my heart beating crazily, and over to Broadway. I found a pay phone right on that corner, double-parked, and ran out. As I dialed, I kept an eye on the car.

It rang a few times, and then Granite's voice came on. "This is H. K. Granite. If you leave your name and number—"

I hung up, went back to the car, and turned onto Broadway, going south. At 106th Street, Broadway bends east, to your left. If you continue straight, you enter West End Avenue. That's what I did. I drove until I found a place to park, then walked to Granite's address. I rang, but there was no answer. I found a corner where I would be out of the way and I waited.

It was nearly an hour before he arrived. He entered the outer foyer without seeing me and went straight to the locked door with his key.

"Mr. Granite."

He turned abruptly. It took a moment before he recognized me. "What do you want?" he asked brusquely.

"I need to talk to you," I said. "I have a few questions."

"Ask them here. I have things to do upstairs."

"I don't think this is the place."

"I'm a busy man."

"It's about Hannah."

He controlled himself well, but I think he knew that I had found out. In fact, I was the nervous one. All I had was a little arithmetic and a wild guess whose proof was in the past.

He unlocked the door and held it for me without saying anything. During the elevator ride, he was quiet. When we got to his apartment, he dropped his hat and coat on a chair in the foyer but didn't offer to take mine. Again. We went into the living room.

"What do you want to know?"

"I have some questions about Hannah Herskovitz."

"What makes you think I could answer them? I told you, I wasn't even a member of the circle. It was my parents who were."

I took my best shot first. "You were her lover."

He sat down. "Who told you that?" He still sounded belligerent. I wondered what Hannah had seen in him. He was a handsome man, but he had a repelling manner.

I sat down, too. "No one told me. No one would tell me. I figured it out. I want you to confirm it for me. I don't intend to tell anyone."

"We were lovers," he said.

I felt a surge of elation. "When? How long?"

"Long." He turned to look at a piece of sculpture, and his eyes glazed. "The circle started in the late forties, after the Herskovitzes arrived. During the war it had been less formal, more like individual friendships. Nathan seemed to bring them all together. I was in my mid-twenties, but I was still living at home. There weren't any apartments in New York, not for what I could pay, and I was still going to school part-time, working a little, trying to open a gallery. Even after I moved out, I would come home to see my parents once a week and come to the circle when it was at their place. It was fun. I knew them all. And Hannah was there."

I watched him get himself together. He was so impatient, so brusque, I had not imagined anything could affect him this way.

"We met when the circle started. I suppose even then I thought about her in relation to me, not as his wife, but it was a long time before anything happened. They looked like father and daughter to me, not like husband and wife. He was in his forties, she was in her twenties. She was so beautiful, so—light. I finally moved out when I was about thirty. That wasn't unusual then. I had a lot of friends who were working on degrees and living at home in those days. I had a little place downtown in the Village for a while and I used to think about having her down, but she'd had a baby around forty-nine, and I didn't see how it could work. We were friends by then. We'd sit and talk together when the circle met. I knew she felt something. I remember when she was pregnant with the girl, I couldn't believe . . .

"Eventually it happened, that's all. She found somebody to watch the children and she went downtown and we met."

"Why didn't she leave him?" I asked.

"She was afraid of losing the children, and she was afraid . . . Did you know Nathan?"

"A little."

"I thought he'd kill me."

"Literally?"

"Literally. We all knew what was going on between him and Black."

"What was going on?"

"He hounded him, followed him, waited for him outside his house or at the university. Plagued him. Badgered him. Threatened him, I suppose. The guy was eventually found dead in the street of a heart attack. I certainly thought Nathan provoked it."

"Maybe his conscience provoked it, Mr. Granite. Do you have any idea why Nathan didn't try to get the book back through the courts when he got to this country?"

"They used to talk about it at the circle," he said. "They were all willing to testify for him. But he said, 'Here's what Black's lawyer will do. He'll put each of you on the stand and ask, "Did Nathan Herskovitz give you a book?" And you'll say, "Yes." And he'll say, "To keep or as payment for services rendered?" And you'll say, "To keep." And that'll be their defense.' "

"There's certainly a kind of logic in that," I said.

"There was one guy, Aaron Strauss, who could have testified differently for Nathan, but he was never very well, and Nathan didn't want to subject him to being a witness. Or so the story goes."

"So Hannah stayed with Nathan, and you lived by yourself, and you had an affair for a long time."

"That's what happened."

"Why did she kill herself?"

"You know it's none of your damned business."

"I do know that, Mr. Granite. But someone murdered Nathan, and everything that happened to him leads me toward his killer."

"You think I killed him?"

I wanted to say that I thought he was too weak to have done it, but I restrained myself. "Not really. What happened to Hannah?"

"What happened to Hannah is that she got pregnant."

I closed my eyes, feeling pity for her.

"Yes," he said. "That was no picnic in the nineteen fifties. She couldn't have it, although I—There were plenty of reasons why she couldn't go through with it. I got her an abortion, the best you could get."

"Did she want the baby?" I asked.

He thought about it. "I'm not sure."

"But she agreed to the abortion."

"She agreed. And then"—his voice thinned—"she just went into a terrible depression."

"How awful."

"And one day"—he shook his head as though he still didn't understand it—"she did it. It very nearly destroyed me," he said, his voice catching.

"I'm sorry."

"I don't know if anyone knew," he said, his voice a little stronger. "There must have been suspicions. We were very discreet. She was so lovely." He sat with his head down. When he looked up, his face was wet. "The bastard didn't even go to her funeral."

I got up. It was growing dusky in the room. He had not put any lights on when we came in, and some of the sculptures had begun to look like lurking shadows. I put my bag over my shoulder and went to the foyer. He stood and followed me.

"Why did you go to Nathan's funeral?" I asked, my hand on the doorknob.

He looked at me as though I had missed the point of everything. "Without him, I wouldn't be alive today," he said.

23

When I got home, I called Franciotti. He was actually there and he talked to me.

"Glad you called," he said. "I took a clue from something you said yesterday and checked out the keys in Finch's pocket. One of them opens the downstairs door at the building Herskovitz lived in."

It was the best news I had heard all day. "So he could easily have gotten in without breaking in or going over the roof."

"That's probably how he did it. We picked up Angel Ramirez and found a gold tie clip in his pocket with Herskovitz's initials on the back. While Finch was looking for that address book, Angel must've been shopping the place for souvenirs, although Finch obviously didn't want him to."

"How's your case against Jesus holding up?"

There was a pause. "We've got a few loose ends."

So Arnold was right. "What about Angel? Could he have killed Nathan?"

"Also shaky. But he had one hell of a lump on his head when we picked him up."

"I figured he was my man. By the way, did you find any keys belonging to Nathan Herskovitz that might open a safe-deposit box or vault in a bank?"

"Oh yeah, we found that."

"Any old books in the box?" I asked hopefully.

"Nothing but paper and an old wedding ring. He owned some municipals, had some certificates, that kind of thing. No life insurance, in case you care. But I found out something you'll be interested in. I checked back to 1975. Herskovitz's apartment was burglarized—the detective squad file says it was really torn up—but nothing seemed to be missing."

"They were looking for the book."

"Looks that way. And there's something else. About that time a warrant was issued on a complaint by a Mrs. Mildred Black to search Herskovitz's apartment."

"She thought he'd stolen the book."

"But it wasn't there."

"Thanks for the information, Sergeant. I'll keep you posted if I find out anything," I said, wanting to keep our relations cordial.

"I appreciate that, Miss Bennett."

A little after six, Arnold called. From the sounds in the background, I was pretty sure he was still at his office.

"Got a call from Bert Finch today," he said. "Sounds like you've been twisting arms."

"I got tired of being nice and getting nowhere. It seemed to me that Paterno and Nathan stayed in that building to be near each other. If they moved, they had no guarantee they'd get apartments in the same building. Gallagher stayed because they did and because he wouldn't pay an extra dollar if he moved. Once Nathan was gone, Mrs. Paterno wanted to be gone, too, at least from 603. I let Gallagher hear my conversation with Finch so he'd know what I was bargaining for. I think he loved it."

"He should have. It sounds as though he won't have to pay much more than what he's paying now, if what Finch told me is accurate."

"I said ten dollars more a month. Believe me, Arnold, Gallagher can afford it. He's got a pension from the city, Social Security, and savings. He probably gets more a month than I do. He just likes to complain."

"What the hell, he's a New Yorker. That's half the fun."

I was starting to think he was right. "Is Finch going to cooperate?"

"Looks that way. I'll hear from him in the next day or two. But I've got some news for you."

"About what?"

"I got a look at Nathan's will today."

"He wrote a will?" I had never thought about that.

"He was a lawyer, wasn't he? Lawyers write wills."

"Did he have anything to leave?"

"Cash and a bunch of CDs. He left everything to his children."

"His children," I said in amazement.

"Who else do you leave your money to?"

"His daughter considered him dead for twenty years, and he barely spoke to his son."

"Probably all a misunderstanding."

"Probably," I agreed. And then it hit me. "Arnold, what did he leave Amelia Paterno?"

"Not mentioned."

I think it struck us both at the same moment, because we started talking together.

"You think she found out?" he said when I had relinquished the floor.

"And killed him in anger. It's possible. It sure gives us a motive. And she and I went through his apartment together the other day, looking for a missing possible weapon. She said she couldn't see anything missing. If she used it and took it, she sure wouldn't want to identify it."

"Why would he have told her?" Arnold asked.

"Oh, I don't know, Arnold. I don't know why anyone does anything anymore."

"Sounds like you've had a bad day."

"I have. Maybe I'll tell you about it sometime."

"So here we are, sitting on a nice piece of information."

"I'll go see her tomorrow."

"Are you nuts? If she did it to Nathan, she could do it to you."

"I'll tell her you told me. She'll know I'm not the only one who knows."

"You'd better watch yourself, Chrissie."

"I'll watch," I said, thinking I was starting to sound like an elderly New Yorker.

I still had the keys to Mrs. Paterno's apartment. She had not asked for them, and I had decided to keep them in case something happened that might make them evidence in the case. If I told Franciotti I had had them and given them back, they wouldn't be of much use. But I had promised myself I would not use them to enter her apartment.

She wasn't home, and I hoped I wouldn't have to wait all day. If she was delivering sketches somewhere downtown, she might not be back for hours.

I went to see Gallagher and told him that things looked good for a move. He was delighted. Finally I asked him something that had been on my mind for a long time.

"Are you and Mrs. Paterno friendly?"

"Friendly? With that dragon?"

I stifled a smile. "But she gave you her key."

"She had to give it to someone. And I think she wanted the key to Herskovitz's."

"Why?"

He smiled slyly. "Oh, he's got a little more in the bank than me. That counts with Paterno."

"OK, Ian. We'll keep this conversation to ourselves."

"And who would I be tellin'? Do the walls have ears?"

I went back up to six—I was developing real muscles in my calves—but Paterno was still out. I went downstairs and waited in the lobby. About ten minutes later she walked in with a bag of groceries.

"Can I help you with those?" I asked. "I've been waiting to talk to you."

"I can help myself, thank you." She headed for the door to the stairs, and I followed.

We went up to six, Mrs. Paterno lugging the groceries, I holding my flashlight to light her way, something that I think annoyed her.

When we got to her apartment, I went in with her and

waited while she put away what she had bought. When she was finished, I said, "May I take you to lunch today?"

"I can take myself to lunch, but it's too early."

I had thought it might be safer talking to her in a public place, but her living room would have to do.

"Mrs. Paterno," I said when we were more or less comfortable, "Arnold Gold called me yesterday. He's seen Nathan's will."

If it frightened her, she showed nothing.

"Nathan left everything to his children."

I tensed, but my news fell like a wet rag.

"There was no mention of you at all in the will."

"Is that what you came to tell me?"

"I thought somebody should," I said, starting to feel silly.

"I don't know why. I wasn't a member of his family."

"I thought . . ." I was really pushing it now. "I had hoped he'd make some provisions for you. You were friends for so long."

"He did."

"He did?"

"Yes. Is that something I must now discuss with the police? After thirty years of keeping everything quiet and discreet, must we now hang everything out to dry, as they say?"

"No, of course not." I stood up to go. It was too early in the day to feel weary, but this was getting me down. "Just between us, Mrs. Paterno," I said, grasping at straws, "how did Nathan provide for you?"

"He gave me a certificate of deposit for a large sum of money. I argued with him for years about it. I have my work, I have something from my ex-husband." It was the first time she had ever mentioned him to me. "I will have Social Security when I choose to take it, and I am not an extravagant person. But he insisted, and finally he just gave it to me."

"When was this?"

"A month or so ago. I don't remember exactly."

"Would you mind—I'd like very much to see it. I don't care how much it's for. You can cover up the amount."

"It's in my box."

"In the bank?"

"Yes."

"Could we—we have no one, Mrs. Paterno. The case against Ramirez is falling apart. I don't know where to look next. If Nathan was killed over the book, we just don't know who could have done it. People are killed over money every day. Maybe, somehow . . ."

She gave me a hard look, then got up and put her coat on. I had no idea what I was looking for at that point, just that this was a new piece of information, and I had to follow up on it.

We walked over to Broadway and then up to her bank. I waited while she got her box, opened it, removed the certificate, and put the box back. She came over to where I was standing and handed it to me.

All it was, was an ordinary passbook. The conditions were typed on the inside cover, the owners' names, the interest rate, the term. The joint owners were Nathan Herskovitz and Amelia Paterno. The amount was seventy-five thousand dollars. No interest was noted, but the certificate was only four or five weeks old. The certificate had been taken out on September 6. Then it occurred to me. Interest was usually paid at the end of each quarter.

"Shouldn't you have had the interest credited at the end of September?" I asked.

"There isn't any interest. It's sent to him."

"Of course," I said, feeling stupid. "That's what he lived on."

"That's what we all live on."

"And now the checks will be sent to you. Have you notified them that he's—passed away?"

"I never thought of it. The money means nothing to me."

"Why don't you do it now?" I said gently. "It is yours."

She seemed to consider it. "It's another bank," she said.

"I'll walk over with you."

Nathan's bank was the other side of Seventy-ninth Street. On the way down I persuaded her to have lunch. She ate sparingly, a salad and black coffee. When we were done, I grabbed the check and ignored her protests.

We found a young, attractive black officer named Mrs. Dickson at Nathan's bank who was free to help us. She told Mrs. Paterno what proof she would need to have the certificate transferred to her name alone, or to her name and that of her daughter, which was what she wanted.

"Excuse me," I said. "I'm helping out the Herskovitz family since Mr. Herskovitz's death. I understand there are tax complications when someone dies." I knew a little about this because I had inherited all of my aunt Meg's "estate" earlier in the year. "I assume this is money that used to be Mr. Herskovitz's and now will be Mrs. Paterno's."

"Yes," she said.

"Mr. Herskovitz took this certificate out in September. Can you tell me where the money came from?"

"What do you mean?"

"Well, did he write you a check for it or roll over an old certificate?"

She frowned. "I'm not sure . . ."

"Please," I said ingenuously. "It's so important."

In books the detective always has a source he can call at banks and insurance companies and places of employment to get the kind of information you and I aren't privy to. It's true I had Jack in the police department and Arnold to help me with legal matters, but that's hardly enough. I just asked and crossed my fingers that she would accommodate me.

"I'll have to check the computer," she said, and I held my breath.

I guess everyone has a computer nowadays. She turned toward her screen and pressed keys while we waited. There was a lot of keying.

Finally she said, "He rolled over a certificate of the same amount."

"In his name?"

"In his and a Mitchell Herskovitz's."

"To whom did the checks go?" I asked.

"To Nathan Herskovitz. He's the first name on the certificate."

"So you wouldn't have notified Mitchell when the certificate was rolled over in a different name."

"Oh no. This kind of thing happens every day. We only deal with the first person named."

"I see."

Mrs. Paterno got up to go.

"Well, thank you very much," I said.

"But we would have told him about the checking," Mrs. Dickson said.

"What checking?"

She looked back at her screen. "When Mr. Nathan took out the last certificate, we were giving free checking for CDs over fifty thousand dollars. Both Mr. Nathan and Mr. Mitchell got it. When the names changed, Mrs. Paterno here got free checking, and we notified Mr. Mitchell that he would have to start paying for his."

"When would Mitchell have been notified?" I asked, my heart starting to pound uncomfortably.

"About the middle of September. It takes a little time to do the paperwork."

"Let's go," I said to Mrs. Paterno. I thanked Mrs. Dickson and Mrs. Paterno, and I left the bank.

"Do you think . . . ?" she said as we went out to Broadway.

"I don't know what to think."

"I forgot to tell you, I think I know what killed him. I think I know what's missing."

"You do?"

"I went back yesterday by myself and looked around."

"Show me," I said.

24

"It's gone," Mrs. Paterno said.

We were standing in Nathan's living room, in front of the mantelpiece over the boarded-up fireplace. She was right. It was gone. Whenever I had gone to visit Nathan, whenever we sat in the living room, I was conscious of the ticking of the marble clock. It wasn't the absence of Nathan that had made the apartment so quiet; it was the absence of the clock.

"It was very heavy," Mrs. Paterno said. "I think he found it in an antique store a long time ago and had it fixed up. He said it reminded him of one his parents had when he was a boy."

He had told me something quite similar once.

"It's funny we both missed it," she said.

"It wasn't meant to be missed. Someone moved the other things on the mantel, so there wouldn't be a gap. It looks as if it was never there."

"But you couldn't just carry it out under your arm. It was too big and too heavy."

"You could carry it out if you had a suitcase with you, if you were on your way to the airport to fly home."

She stared at me with her dark eyes. "What should we do?"

"I have some phone calls to make. I don't want to use this phone."

"Come upstairs."

I felt a little uneasy. I had no credit anywhere. I was four months out of a convent where I earned in the high two figures each month—and gave some of it to charity.

"The calls may be expensive," I said hesitantly. "I don't have a credit card to charge them to."

She looked at me witheringly. "I am not Mr. Gallagher," she said. "I want to find out who killed Nathan as much as you do."

We went upstairs and I called St. Stephen's. Grace was on bells, and we made a little small talk before I asked her my question.

"Do you have the name of that travel agent that we always use at St. Stephen's?"

"Yes, it's Emily at Round the World. Do you want her number?"

"Please."

I wrote it down, sent my regards to everyone, and hung up. Then I dialed Round the World and asked for Emily.

"Emily," I said when she came on the line, "this is Chris Bennett. I used to be at St. Stephen's. I was Sister Edward Frances."

"Sister Edward," she said cordially. "I didn't know you'd left."

"A few months ago. Emily, I have to ask you a favor." I explained the situation. When she heard it was a murder, there was nothing she wouldn't do for me. "I have to find out whether a man named Mitchell Herskovitz flew from New York to Atlanta on September twenty-ninth, late afternoon or evening, or September thirtieth in the morning. Can you do that?"

"I sure can. I'll make like I'm his travel agent. You know, I call a special number that's only for agents. Right away that gives me access that you can't get."

"Great. And while you're at it, it might be helpful if I knew where he came from when he flew into New York."

"Easy once I find out if he was booked New York to Atlanta. It may take me some time, Sister—uh—"

"Chris."

"Chris, of course. I have a lot of airlines and a lot of flights to check, and I've got to leave early today. Can I call you tomorrow morning?"

"I'll wait at home for your call." I gave her my number, and we hung up.

"Do you think he came up here to kill his father?" Mrs. Paterno asked.

"No, I don't. I think he probably never knew that Nathan had him listed on certificates. My aunt listed me on some of hers, and I didn't know it till she died and I found them in the safe-deposit box. But he knew about that one because of the free checking. When he heard from the bank that the checking was no longer free, he thought Nathan was taking the money away from him, or something like that. Maybe he thought he was being completely disinherited. He may have had a business trip to New York and decided to ask his father what happened."

"And they had a fight."

I shook my head. "It wasn't a fight. It was really something very tragic."

I left her and drove home, arriving before four. I felt sick and worried and discouraged. I called Sergeant Franciotti, but he was off. He would be in tomorrow.

Then I called Jack.

"Hi, how's things?" he asked when he got on the phone.

"I need your help," I said.

"What's wrong? You sound terrible."

"Jack, if I discover evidence pointing to a possible murderer, do I tell his lawyer or do I tell the police? There's a house that has to be searched, and somebody has to get a warrant. Would the lawyer see to that?"

"What happened?" he said, his manner all official.

"I can't tell you now. I'll tell you tomorrow. I'm just afraid that—I want to tell Arnold, but I don't want to compromise him. He's the attorney for my suspect."

He didn't answer right away. Somehow I knew he wouldn't go after Arnold this time. "I'll ask my law professor tonight. I'll have an answer for you when I get home. Is ten too late to call?"

"I'll wait up. I have to know, Jack. I have to do the right thing."

* * *

It was after ten when he called. I was in bed reading, and I turned so quickly to answer that I lost my place.

"I got it," he said.

"Yes."

"You know lawyers; they sit on the fence." I wondered when the turning point would come, when his sympathies would cross the line, in favor rather than against. "I put it to him the way you explained it. He said it's a judgment call. The attorney might thwart the search for any evidence that would tend to incriminate his client. My guess is that Gold would take that position, from what I know of him. When I suggested turning the evidence over to the police, the professor said, 'That's a much better idea. They can get the search going on probable cause. We have a crime, a suspect, and probable cause to believe that something will be found in a certain place based on information or a strong likelihood.' That's it."

"I'll call Franciotti tomorrow, if I have anything."

"You really think you're close?"

"I won't know till tomorrow."

"If you need a warrant, do it before Saturday. They only issue them on weekdays. And cross your fingers for a sympathetic judge."

"Thanks."

"You still want me to meet you at the Herskovitz place?"

"I'll be there Saturday, in any event."

I walked early on Friday, meeting no one. Then I went back for breakfast and a long wait. Emily didn't call until almost noon.

"I've got it," she said triumphantly. "The problem was, when I finally found the airline, it turned out he missed his connection Friday afternoon, New York to Atlanta, and he had to change airlines. When he got out to the airport, he was standby, but that was a very busy night. It was Friday, which is always heavy, but it was also a Jewish holiday."

"I know," I said. "Yom Kippur."

"That's it. He finally got on a late flight with Delta. Do you want the details?"

"Please." I wrote them down.

"He arrived in New York early Friday from Philadelphia."

"He must have been on a business trip," I said.

"The whole trip was charged to his company's travel agent."

"I really appreciate it, Emily."

"Oh, gosh, it was a pleasure. Is this your murderer?"

"I hope not," I said.

Franciotti wasn't in. What a surprise. I wondered briefly where detectives go when they're "out." I left my name and number and said it was urgent. That hadn't done much good on Monday when Bettina and I had our little adventure, but I felt we were on friendlier terms now. I called again at two, but he was still out.

I started to get nervous. Jack had said you couldn't get a warrant on Saturday, and I just couldn't see waiting till Monday to put this to rest. Besides, I wanted Franciotti to check something at Nathan's apartment before the Herskovitzes came in and started packing.

It was four when he got back to me. I told him what I had learned, down to the flight numbers.

"Jeez, you mean the son?" he said.

"It looks that way. He spent the previous night in Philadelphia, so he probably had a suitcase with him. If his clothes were bloody, he could easily have changed in the apartment, even if he put on yesterday's dirty shirt. And we finally figured out what's missing from the living room, a heavy marble clock."

"Aha," Franciotti said. "Which he could have taken with him in the suitcase. Sounds like you've got a lot of solid facts there. Nice."

"I think someone in Atlanta ought to get a warrant and search his house. They may find the clock stashed somewhere, and the bloody clothes, too. It's not likely he dropped them in the laundry."

"I'll get right on it."

"Sergeant, Mitchell and his wife are flying in tonight. I don't know where they're staying, but their children might. If the house is searched tonight, they may call him and warn him."

"I'll tell Atlanta to get the warrant and hold off executing it till tomorrow. The search can wait a day."

"Good idea," I said, as though it had been his. "There's something else you may want to look into." I took a deep breath and admitted to him that I had looked around the apartment that day last week when he had found me there, the day after the break-in. "I wore the big yellow rubber gloves that hang over the pail under the kitchen sink. It occurred to me that if the killer came into the kitchen to wash or wipe off his hands, he might have seen those gloves and put them on to rearrange the things on the mantel. I know that my handling them kind of bollixes things up, but maybe you could get some prints off them. And I'm sure any man's fingers are longer and thicker than mine. They may have left some prints."

"Good thinking. I'll go over there with a lab guy as soon as I talk to Atlanta."

I didn't want to hold him up on his call, but something was still niggling at me. "There's just one more thing," I said. "When Mrs. Paterno and I went into the apartment the day we found the body, she was absolutely sure the bolt was locked. It means the killer had a key."

"Or she remembered wrong. Mitchell Herskovitz is supposed to pick up the keys to his father's place tomorrow morning. I have a note about it."

"I just wanted you to know."

"Thanks. Let me call Atlanta."

25

Saturday was not the best day of my life. I called Arnold in the morning and asked where he would be in the afternoon. He said at home till four or five; they had one of those damned cocktail parties to go to, and they hadn't decided whether to go early and leave early or go late and leave early. I said I might need him.

"Something cooking?"

"You know me," I said lightly. "There's always something cooking."

"By the way, I talked to Bert Finch yesterday. He's got apartments in two different buildings for Gallagher and Paterno, ready for inspection. He'll paint to suit."

"That's really wonderful, Arnold. I'll tell them when I go down this afternoon."

"Mitchell cleaning the place out?"

"He should be."

I tried Franciotti, but he wasn't at the precinct squad. I checked with Celia, and she said she would wait up for me. I promised not to be too late. Then I packed a bag.

I had already decided to leave Celia's early on Sunday and not attend mass with her. I stopped going on a weekly basis after I left St. Stephen's, something I was working out for myself. So I packed some casual clothes for the next day and I dropped Mark's prayer book in, in case I had time to leave it off. Then I dressed for my evening. At one I drove into New York.

I carried my overnight bag using the shoulder strap. You can't leave anything that looks like luggage in a parked car because it'll be broken into, and the repair is likely to cost more than replacing what was stolen.

I walked up to Broadway to find a pay phone, and I called Franciotti.

"We got the gloves," he said. "Is Herskovitz in the apartment?"

"I haven't been up there yet, but I would guess so. He told me he wanted to get an early start."

"He never picked up the keys."

"I see. What about Atlanta?"

"I'm waiting on a call from them. Hold on . . . There it is now. I'll see you at the apartment in an hour, one way or the other."

I took out another quarter and dialed the number for St. Luke's Hospital, just to kill a little time before going to Nathan's.

"We expect Mr. Greenspan to be released tomorrow," I was told. I sent my happy good wishes and hung up.

Then I called Arnold. "I'd like you to come to Nathan's apartment," I said when he answered. "There's someone I'd like you to meet."

"Be there in an hour," he said.

I stopped at Gallagher's apartment and told him the good news. He was ecstatic. Then I went up to six and told Mrs. Paterno. She took it the way she took everything, like a neutral weather report. Then I walked down to five.

The door was ajar, but I knocked and called before walking in. As I passed the study, I could see that all the books were gone from the shelves and a number of cartons were stacked in the middle of the room. Mitchell and his wife were in the living room, he in a sport shirt, she in jeans and a big shirt tied in a knot at her waist. We were introduced, and I put on the biggest act of my life. They were wrapping the pictures of Renata and the children in paper that looked as if it had been left by the same mover that had delivered the cartons.

At a quarter to three, Arnold arrived. He's kind of a striking-looking man, tall and lanky with a shock of white hair and one of those lean faces with lots of angles and thick white eyebrows. We all talked a little more while the Herskovitzes worked. Then, just at three, Sergeant Franciotti, his partner, and a uniformed policeman walked through the door.

"Afternoon, Miss Bennett," he said rather formally. He walked by us, holding his shield up, and stopped in front of Mitchell. "Mr. Herskovitz, I'm sorry, but I have to arrest you for the murder of your father, Nathan Herskovitz."

Carolyn screamed, "What?" and Mitchell turned so pale, I was afraid he might faint.

Arnold, of course, retained his cool. "Don't say anything, Mitchell," he said, walking toward him and dodging cartons while Franciotti took handcuffs out of his pocket and started reading Mitchell his rights from his Miranda card. "Sergeant, Mr. Herskovitz is represented by counsel at this time, and there will be no questioning of my client. Now, what's this all about?"

"Acting on a warrant issued in the state of Georgia, the Atlanta police searched Mr. Herskovitz's house this morning"—here Carolyn gasped and covered her mouth with her hands—"where they found a probable murder weapon and a bloodstained shirt."

Mitchell murmured, "Oh, my God," and Arnold looked sternly at me. I nodded, feeling as miserable as I have ever felt.

"I only came to see if he was all right," Mitchell said with a sob in his voice. "He took my name off a certificate, and I thought he was getting forgetful. I thought maybe he needed some help. And then we came in here and I saw the pictures and I just couldn't bear it. I didn't know what I was doing. I just knew I had to do something, something for my mother's sake. My poor mother, my poor, poor mother who lived with that—"

But Arnold was practically shouting through Mitchell's impassioned monologue. "Don't say anything, Mitchell. Nothing, not a word. Mr. Herskovitz has no statement to make, Sergeant."

When Mitchell had calmed down, Arnold spoke briefly and quietly to him, and I went to comfort Carolyn, who was beyond comforting. Franciotti's partner and the uniformed policeman took Mitchell away, but Franciotti stayed.

"We'll get some prints off those gloves," he said to me, "and match 'em after Herskovitz gets printed. When the lab does its job on the shirt, we'll compare the blood type with the father's. You were right about everything in the house in Atlanta."

"I wish I hadn't been."

"You want to explain?" Arnold said.

I introduced him to Franciotti, and then I went quickly through what I had learned in the last two days.

"You could've called me," Arnold said.

"I couldn't. I asked Jack what I should do, and he asked his law professor Thursday night. The professor said a suspect's lawyer might not cooperate, to protect his client. If I wanted a search, the police were the best people to tell. I called the sergeant."

"You can't call it murder, Chrissie."

"I know."

I heard the door open and went to see who was there. Jack was coming down the hall, looking gorgeous with a fresh haircut. I put my arms around him and tried to calm myself.

"Trouble?" he said.

"They just arrested Mitchell."

"Shit." He kissed me and let me go, then went to the living room and over to Franciotti. "Sergeant Jack Brooks, Six-Five." He held out his hand.

"Franciotti." He looked from Jack to me and said, "Aha."

I smiled for the first time that day. Then I took Jack over to Arnold.

I could tell as they looked at each other that everything would be all right. Arnold's eyes were piercing, but his lips had a little smile.

"This is Jack," I said. "This is Arnold Gold."

They shook hands, both of them looking pretty pleased.

"Nice to meet you," Jack said. "Don't get this close to a hero very often." I could have kissed him.

"Not a word that's in my vocabulary," Arnold said. "Chrissie tells me you're in training for the noble profession."

"It's a long way off."

"So's Christmas, but it comes around. What are you taking these days?"

When I heard the word "torts," I moved away. Carolyn Herskovitz was sitting in a chair, staring out the window.

"He's a very good lawyer," I said to her. "Mitchell couldn't be in better hands."

"But he couldn't have done it," she cried. "He was in Philadelphia. He *called* me from there."

"I know."

"Hello?" a woman's voice called tunefully, and Mrs. Paterno walked into the room. "Is this what you're looking for?" she asked. She was holding a package wrapped in brown paper and tied with strong cord. I could see Nathan's bold handwriting on the top side.

"What is it?" I asked.

"I have no idea. He gave it to me years ago. He said, 'Just keep it for me.' And I forgot about it."

We opened it together. There was a wooden box inside with hinges and a clasp. Inside there were layers and layers of wrapping, the last one silk. Inside that was a book, a very, very old book with geometric designs on the cover.

We were looking at the Guadalaxara Haggadah.

26

Jack carried my overnight bag over one shoulder and held my arm with his other hand as we walked out into the street.

"Where's your car?" he asked.

"On Riverside Drive. Where's yours?"

"In Brooklyn. I took the subway."

I looked at him.

"I'll show you where I live." He put my bag in the back-seat. "Mind if I drive?"

"Can you drive a shift car?"

"I can drive anything with wheels."

I gave him my keys, sat back, and closed my eyes for a minute. He was right. He could drive anything.

"There were so many things going," I said finally.

"Sounds like it. And they didn't have much to do with each other."

"But in a way, they did. Bert Finch wanted to scare me to death so that I'd get Paterno and Gallagher to leave 603. In a way, he succeeded. I put pressure on them and they agreed."

"But it cost him."

"Oh yes, it cost him. Arnold thought I hammered out a pretty tough deal."

"And when Herskovitz was murdered, it gave the other Finch the idea of moving in on the book."

"He'd been calling Nathan, trying to get him to make a deal, without even knowing for sure that he had the book. Did you see that book, Jack?"

"I was afraid to breathe near it."

201

We had all agreed that the book belonged to Mrs. Paterno, who seemed nonplussed at the idea. When we were leaving, she said something about donating it to a museum in Nathan's memory. I liked that. It made me like her, too.

"Warren Finch knew Nathan didn't have it, or wouldn't keep it where it could be found. He'd staged a break-in fifteen years ago; at least I think he's the one that did it. That was before Metropolitan owned the building. I bet he got his brothers to buy the building so he could have access to Nathan."

"Good thought," Jack said.

"And he probably got it in his head that Nathan kept up with all the people he'd given books to before the war. If he couldn't have 'the big one,' at least he could try for some of the others. That's why he stole the address book."

"And started calling everyone in it."

"Of course, Mrs. Paterno's name wouldn't be there. Nathan was too careful for that. I almost wish Warren Finch had called her. She could really have put him in his place."

"Your friend, the dragon lady."

I laughed. "That's just what Gallagher called her."

"Tell me, how many Ramirezes were there?"

"Two brothers, Angel and Jesus, if you can believe that," I said, pronouncing the names in English.

"Well, they were good boys. You said they went to Puerto Rico to see their sick mother."

"I guess that's one way of looking at it." I kind of sighed. "They were both in Puerto Rico. Jesus came back first and got arrested for the murder. Angel came back a couple of days later and started following me. Then Warren Finch bailed Jesus out of jail last Monday morning, and they both ended up at Bettina Strauss's apartment."

"You're lucky to be alive."

"I know. Maybe you can give me some lessons in hand-to-hand combat."

"You inviting me?"

"Asking you."

He grinned. "Fine. We'll set up a date."

He had worked his way south and east, and we were approaching the Brooklyn Bridge. I had never crossed it before, but there's no mistaking it. It's big and powerful, and you just know it's going to last forever.

"Some view," I said.

Jack reached over and squeezed my hand. "That leaves us with the homicide. I figure Arnold'll get the charge reduced if the DA goes for murder." It was the first time he had called Arnold by his first name.

"It wasn't murder." I could see that living room as we had found it on Yom Kippur morning, two weeks ago, the body of Nathan in his overcoat, his hat a few feet away, blood everywhere. A chill passed through me. "Nathan was a strange, wonderful man," I said. "As his son told me, he had his dark side. From everything I've heard, he hounded a man to death."

"That professor? Sounded like the guy deserved what he got."

"Even so, think of the kind of man that dedicates almost twenty years of his life to something like that."

"He had good reasons."

"He also thought he had good reasons to keep his first family a secret from the children of his second wife."

"I don't think it went that way," Jack said. "You don't tell a three-year-old or a six-year-old that Daddy had a wife before your Mommy. You wait until the kid is older, when he can understand."

"And by the time they could understand, he had alienated them because he was protecting Hannah."

"Makes sense, doesn't it?"

It did. I thought about it as he drove through the narrow streets of Brooklyn Heights with its restored brownstones and pretty trees. "And later, when Hannah was gone and the children were all but gone, he took out the pictures of the people who had never disappointed him. That's what Nina said, the children who would have been stars." I shook my head. "If he had told his children about Renata, he'd be alive today."

"Think so?"

"I'm sure of it. I think what happened is that Mitchell got word from the bank that Nathan had changed the ownership of the certificate, and he came up to see what was going on. His father was old, maybe he was getting forgetful. Mitchell didn't necessarily have any evil intent. He probably met Nathan coming home from his afternoon in the sun and went upstairs with him. He said when I met him that he hadn't been in that apartment for ten years. The day before Yom Kippur was probably that first time. He walked into the living room with his father and saw those pictures. I saw what happened to him when he saw them the Monday after the murder. He put on a good show for me."

"You think he became enraged," Jack said as he slipped into a parking space about six inches longer than my car.

"He realized this had been another family of Nathan's, and he imagined, the way Nina did, that they were the cause of Nathan's 'neglect' of their mother. Of course, he wasn't neglecting her. She was neglecting him. And he protected her honor till he died."

"You going to tell Nina and Mitchell?"

I had worried about that for several days. If I told, Nina might feel more kindly toward her father. But was it my place to overrule him? "I don't think so," I said. "Maybe they'll get some comfort out of the fact that he left everything he owned to them."

"Except the book."

"Yes, except the book."

"I think he'd be proud of you, kid."

I swallowed hard but didn't say anything.

27

His apartment was on the top floor of a brownstone. It was tiny, compact, and so neat, it made me a little ashamed of the loose way I kept my house. I wondered whether he always kept it this way or if it was because he was showing it off to me.

"I love it," I said. "Look at that marvelous kitchen." It was minuscule but very up-to-date.

"Small but serviceable." He took his gun out of the ankle holster he carried it in and put it on a shelf in the coat closet. Then he lifted a strip of Velcro and slipped off the leather holster.

"A self-cleaning oven. I really envy you."

"Say a couple of rosaries for that."

I put my bag down on a chair, and he took me in his arms. It all dissolved, Mitchell, the afternoon, the apartment at 603.

"Call Sister What's-her-name and tell her you're not staying over."

Funny things fluttered inside me.

"Come on," he said in a low voice. "It's time."

As he said it, I knew he was right. It was time. I went to the phone in the kitchen and dialed Celia. I told her I had decided to go home after all, and thanks anyway. She said she would miss my visit. I hung up and stood looking at the phone.

"You don't like to lie, do you?"

I shook my head.

"Look at it this way. If we're both here, it's home."

I liked that. "OK."

Then he kissed me as if he really meant it and started unbuttoning my jacket.

For fifteen years, nearly half my life, I had lived a very structured life. Rise at five for chapel at five-thirty. Breakfast. Morning activities. Lunch. And on through the day. Few idle moments. Fatigue by early evening, bed generally by nine. Even having a special close friend among the nuns was discouraged for fairly obvious reasons.

Some of that stays with you after you leave. You find yourself planning when this will happen and when that should be done. Since I had left St. Stephen's, nothing had happened the way I had thought it would, and standing on the threshold of Jack's bedroom, I knew it was better this way, better to do something when the time was right than when you had thought the time might be right.

Until last summer, I had not looked at myself in a mirror for fifteen years. Now Jack was about to see the body I had only recently seen myself. But if I had any sense of hesitancy, it evaporated quickly in the heat of a newly overpowering feeling.

His bedroom was very small, with a double bed made up without a spread. The blanket was a bright, deep blue, and the sheets pure white. There were two pillows side by side, and the linen looked freshly ironed. After a first glance, I didn't see very much or care very much what the room looked like or what a structured life offered or what good planning could do for you. I let the rest of me take over.

It was quite lovely.

It was dark, and I think Jack had fallen asleep briefly. He stirred and said, "Hungry?"

I said, "Not anymore," and he said, "I didn't mean that," and I said, "I didn't mean that either."

We got up and dressed, sort of, and he took two steaks out of the refrigerator that looked as though they could have fed the whole house. When I objected to the size, he cut one in half and said I should take it home with me tomorrow.

He was a lot better than I at cooking. He microwaved a mixture of fresh vegetables and made a salad. With balsamic vinegar.

"What is a cop doing with balsamic vinegar?" I asked.

"My sister the caterer gave it to me for my birthday," he said. "Tastes just like ordinary."

I laughed. I just liked the idea of having a sister. I was an only child who lost her father very young and her mother at fourteen. It's a loss I never completely got over.

It was a great meal, a time to set aside the murder and the loss, my anguish at Mitchell's role. There was something different about us as we sat at adjoining sides of his small table, eating his great dinner. For the first time since I met him, I felt completely comfortable with him.

I was, needless to say, awake early. When it got light, Jack woke up.

"You like to walk in the morning?" he asked.

"I do almost every day."

"Let's do it."

He gave me a sweatshirt to put on over my plaid flannel shirt so I could go without a coat on, since my jacket was home in Oakwood. We walked over to the river and then alongside it toward the Statue of Liberty. There were walkers and runners everywhere, singles, couples of all kinds, fathers and children. It was a glorious day. Wherever you looked, it was beautiful. Just across the river was the southern end of Manhattan with all the buildings that make up the skyline. After a while we stopped and looked out over the water, feeling the wind.

That's when I remembered. "I have to do something," I said. "For Nathan. In Manhattan."

"Can it wait till after breakfast?"

"Yes." I walked over to the grassy area on the other side of the walkway. "I need some stones."

"Rocks?"

"Yes."

"How big?"

"A couple of big ones. The rest, it doesn't matter."

We went looking for them, going back toward our starting point. The little ones were easy; they were everywhere. It took some doing to find the big ones. We got back to Jack's place laden.

"You gonna tell me about it?"

"After breakfast."

It was near noon when we got to West Seventy-ninth Street. From Riverside Drive we walked down to the boat basin at the western end of Seventy-ninth. Some people actually live on boats that are docked there. Others keep their boats for weekend use. It's a pretty place, and from that point you can walk either north or south right along the Hudson River. I hadn't known that, but policemen seem to be very knowledgeable about their city.

We went down below the basin. Jack was carrying a small burlap bag he'd found in a kitchen cabinet and filled with our rock collection.

"Wait here," I said. "I have to do this alone."

I took the bag of rocks and carried it in my arms. *Every man's death diminishes me,* I thought as I walked, but especially this one. About fifty feet from where I'd left Jack, I stopped, put the bag down, and opened my handbag. Inside, along with the flashlight, which I wouldn't have to carry much longer, and the roll of quarters, which I might be able to dispense with, too, I found Mark Brownstein's prayer book. I turned the pages until I came to the one with his favorite writing: "Inscribe me for blessing in the Book of Life." Sadly, it was too late for that. I turned a few more pages until I found what I wanted.

I leaned against the railing with my right side and faced south. I didn't know how the Jews did it or how Nathan had planned to do it, so I did it the way it seemed right to me.

"This is for Nathan," I said. I believe in saying things aloud. Then there's no question about whether you thought it or thought you thought it. It was spoken.

"For the sin which we have sinned against Thee under stress or through choice," I read, and I reached into the bag and threw one small stone into the river. "For the sin which we have sinned against Thee openly or in secret." I threw another stone into the river. "For the sin which we have sinned against Thee in stubbornness or in error." And I threw a third rock, a slightly bigger one, into the Hudson.

I went down through the whole list—evil meditations, word of mouth, abuse of power, profanation, a few others—and threw a stone into the river for each one. They were the kinds of sins I had once taken very seriously. Today they didn't seem very important at all.

"And for all the others," I said, thinking of sins that Nathan alone could enumerate, "please forgive him." I picked up the burlap bag and dropped it in the river. It sank quickly.

The day was still beautiful. I could go home now if I chose to and read some poetry, prepare for my Tuesday class, call Joseph and tell her how it had all turned out. There were just so many hours left in the day, and I could fill them all with worthwhile activities.

Or I could go back to Brooklyn with Jack, read the Sunday paper with him, cook dinner while he worked on his law assignments. I could even stay overnight and go home tomorrow. I wasn't needed anywhere. I had a whole, wonderful day of unscheduled hours ahead of me.

"Good-bye, Nathan," I said to the shimmering river. I put the prayer book in my bag and walked back to where my lover waited for me.

About the Author

Lee Harris is the pseudonym for an author who has written several works of fiction under a different name. *The Yom Kippur Murder* is the second book in this series.

Look for these Christine Bennett mysteries by

LEE HARRIS

**in your local bookstore.
Published by Fawcett Books.**